ONCE BITTEN

Julia had been betrayed once in a manner which neither she nor the world would ever forget.

Her brief marriage to the odious Sir Edwin Fitzroy had been abruptly ended when that ungentlemanly gentleman unjustly accused her of adultery. Sir Edwin emerged with both a divorce and her dowry, while Julia was left an outcast from society.

Now, however, Julia was once more an object of desire, with a fortune that made her person worth its weight in gold. This time, she vowed, she would not be fooled. Never again would any man obtain her affections or her property.

That was before she met the handsome, charming, infamous Lord Aylsford, who made it so tempting to break every vow . . . even though she knew he might break her heart. . . .

About the Author

Ellen Fitzgerald is a pseudonym for a well-known romance writer. A graduate of the University of Southern California with a B.A. in English and an M.A. in Drama, Ms. Fitzgerald has also attended Yale University and has had numerous plays produced throughout the country. In her spare time, she designs and sells jewelry. Ms. Fitzgerald lives in New York City.

Dear Reader:

As you know, Signet is proud to keep bringing you the best in romance and now we're happy to announce that we are now presenting you with even more of what you love!

The Regency has long been one of the most popular settings for romances and it's easy to see why. It was an age of elegance and opulence, of wickedness and wit. It was also a time of tumultuous change, the beginning of the modern age and the end of illusion, when money began to mean as much as birth, but still an age when manners often meant more than morality.

Now Signet has commissioned some of its finest authors to write some bigger romances—longer, lusher, more exquisitely sensuous than ever before—wonderful love stories that encompass even more of the flavor of this glittering and flamboyant age. We are calling them "Super Regencies" because they have been liberated from category conventions and have the room to take the Regency novel even further—to the limits of the Regency itself.

Because we want to bring you only the very best, we are publishing these books only on an occasional basis, only when we feel that we can bring you something special. The first of the Super Regencies, *Love in Disguise* by Edith Layton, was published in August to rave reviews and has won two awards. It was followed by two other outstanding titles, *The Guarded Heart* by Barbara Hazard, published in October and *Indigo Moon* by Patricia Rice, published in February. Watch for future Signet Super Regencies in upcoming months in your favorite bookstore.

Sincerely,

Hilary Ross
Associate Executive Editor

Julia's Portion

Ellen Fitzgerald

A SIGNET BOOK

NEW AMERICAN LIBRARY

NAL BOOKS ARE AVAILABLE AT QUANTITY DISCOUNTS WHEN USED TO
PROMOTE PRODUCTS OR SERVICES. FOR INFORMATION PLEASE WRITE TO
PREMIUM MARKETING DIVISION, NEW AMERICAN LIBRARY,
1633 BROADWAY, NEW YORK, NEW YORK 10019.

SIGNET TRADEMARK REG. U.S.PAT. OFF. AND FOREIGN COUNTRIES
REGISTERED TRADEMARK—MARCA REGISTRADA
HECHO EN CHICAGO, U.S.A.

SIGNET, SIGNET CLASSIC, MENTOR, ONYX, PLUME,
MERIDIAN and NAL BOOKS are published by
NAL PENGUIN INC., 1633 Broadway, New York, New York 10019

First Printing, April, 1988

1 2 3 4 5 6 7 8 9

PRINTED IN THE UNITED STATES OF AMERICA

Prologue

The hearing was private, held in the judge's chambers. That much, Sir Henry Carleton, the defendant's father, had been able to arrange. However, Sir Francis Clavering, the judge, did not appear any less forbidding to young Lady Fitzroy, who, decorously clad in black and flanked by her father and her eldest brother, Raymond, sat quietly listening to the testimony of one Sir James Massinger, a man she barely remembered, speaking of events she did not remember at all!

She did remember the opera ball with its masses of laughing and, more often than not, screaming people. There had been music and dancing and an astonishing array of costumes. She had noted sailors, Hindus, Egyptian princesses, clowns, scores of monks and nuns, none of these acting in a manner conforming with their sober habits. Her escort, Sir Markham Caswell, had worn a black domino, and Sir James Massinger, she rather thought, had been similarly clad. The man she had reluctantly called husband for the last two months —Sir Edwin Fitzroy—had not been present.

"It is best that you go with Mark, my dear," he had said on that fatal night. "I find these masquerades a dead bore. I will go early to bed, I think."

Those were, she thought suddenly, among the last words they had exchanged. She darted a glance at Sir Edwin. He appeared stern and self-righteous. It was an expression he had been wearing ever since Sir James Massinger had brought her home on that never-to-be-forgotten morning a month earlier.

Sir James had just begun his deposition. He had followed Sir Markham Caswell, who had described bringing her to the ball and taking her to one of the boxes overlooking the vast auditorium. She did remember that.

She glanced at Sir Francis and winced. The judge looked as if he had eaten something disagreeable. Opera balls, given at the Italian Opera House, were known to be disreputable. Only, she had not known it. Neither Sir Markham nor her husband had informed her of that fact. Indeed, the whole idea of a costume and mask had been incredibly exciting, and Edwin, Sir Markham had assured her, was much in favor of the idea. She had received similar assurances from her husband. Consequently, his recent testimony concerning his shock at his wife's attending such a function was extremely confusing.

Once more her gaze strayed to her husband's face. She had never admired his appearance. His pale blue eyes were too small and his mouth was also small. His nose had a bump in the middle and his hair was a mousy brown. Though Parks, his valet, had done his best to help him achieve a fashionable coiffure, the effect was less than flattering. Indeed, the whole effect was horrid! He himself was also horrid in ways that she longed to forget but could not quite erase from her mind.

In point of fact, she was remembering her wedding night and, as usual, she shuddered. She had known him less than two months when they were married and she had known nothing at all about what her sister Eliza had delicately described as "the duties of a wife."

Her sister had taken her aside on her wedding day and had muttered something about the various intimacies of marriage. She had not been very explicit and she had blushed a great deal as she said, "You must not be surprised at anything a gentleman does when you are together." Eliza had left her confused and curious. Sir Edwin had, at least, assuaged her curiosity that same evening. She shrank from remembering that evening— but inexorably it seemed to roll behind her eyes like the pictures in a panorama.

Once her abigail had undressed her and arrayed her in a long lacy nightgown and had settled her in bed, Sir Edwin had entered the room. Much to her surprise, he had been wearing a long white nightshirt. Summarily dismissing the girl, he had, to her extreme surprise, joined her in bed, and laughing at her shy protests, had visited horrid wet kisses on her lips. Subsequently he had done all manner of things that had disgusted and astonished her, leaving her at the last in considerable pain. There had not been a repetition of those acts. He had left her alone, giving her the impression that she had not pleased him.

He had not pleased her either. He had never pleased her. She had been only ten months past her sixteenth birthday when her mother had told her she was betrothed to him. The marriage, she had explained, would take place a fortnight past her seventeenth birthday. She had alternately stormed and sobbed, begging her parents not to make her marry a man she had seen but twice in her life. Inexorably her mother had pointed out that it was all arranged. She had been reminded that the marriages of her two brothers and two sisters had also been arranged by their parents—or, more specifically, their mother. Lady Carleton had not needed to point out that she was particularly eager to be rid of her youngest daughter.

Julia heaved a sigh. Her mother had never really liked her. She laid her ill health directly at her door—as if,

indeed, it were her fault that she had been born when
her mother was forty-two, well past the age of comfortable childbearing. She had never forgiven Julia for that
ill-timed arrival, and her main ambition in life was to
marry her off as soon as she could find someone who
would come up to scratch.

Julia paused in her recollections. Sir James was now
describing that moment when he had taken her back to
his lodgings. She did not remember that. She did
remember that Sir Mark had left the box. He had
informed her that he had sighted an old friend three
boxes away, and after greeting him, would return immediately. Then, when she was beginning to believe he
would never return, Sir James had arrived and asked her
if she wanted something to drink. She had already
quaffed a large amount of champagne and she had
really wanted to join the dancers on the floor below—
but Sir James had given her something that made her
feel very light-headed. She had been so light-headed, in
fact, that she had not even remembered leaving the
opera house. In fact, she had not remembered anything
of the evening until she awakened the following
morning in his bed! Subsequently he had, upon learning
her direction, taken her back to Edwin. Her husband
had denounced her as a Jezebel and a whore—and demanded the divorce which was now in the process of
taking place . . . But she must listen to what Sir James
was saying!

"She asked me if I would take her out of the ball-
room. She said it was so noisy she could not hear herself
think. I, of course, assented. I asked her her direction
but she said she wanted to go home with me. She said
that her escort had deserted her because they had quar-
reled. She hinted that it had been a lovers' quarrel.
Well . . ." Sir James smiled briefly. "What was I to do?
I did not find her unattractive, and since she was im-

ploring me to take her to my lodgings, I yielded. I will
say that I was already a trifle foxed . . . else I must have
exercised more caution. On coming to my lodgings . . .
well''—a slight smile flitted across his face—''I expect I
must spare the lady's blushes. Suffice to say that the
subsequent happenings were . . . mutually agreeable, or
so she led me to imagine. In the morning, it was a
different story. She was all tears and protestations
concerning her *husband*. I was shocked. However, I had
perforce to bring her home and explain the situation. I
expected he would call me out . . . but he was surprisingly understanding. And this, your honor, is the truth
about that evening. I cannot lie and say I did not comply
with the young lady's earnest supplications. She is a
pretty armful, after all.''

"That is quite enough, Sir James. You have already
made your point on that count," Sir Francis said in
tones of disgust. He fastened a cold, measuring eye on
the defendant. "As for you, young woman, have you
anything to add to this sorry tale?"

Julie swallowed a lump in her throat. Judging from
the magistrate's demeanor, he had already made up his
mind regarding the events of that evening. She said in a
small voice, "I can only say, as I have said before, your
honor, that I have no recollection of the evening. I
remember only being in the box at the opera house and
waking the next morning in Sir James's lodgings. All
else is a blank to me."

The judge glared at her. "You will please stand," he
said icily. As Julie got to her feet, he continued in tones
of disdain, "I have heard the testimony of two worthy
gentlemen: Sir Markham Caswell and Sir James
Massinger. I have also heard the testimony of Sir Edwin
Fitzroy, your unfortunate young husband. You, too,
are young. I will say, Lady Fitzroy, that in all my years
on the bench, I have seldom met so bold and so accom-

plished a liar as yourself—and at so youthful an age. I
am shocked and disgusted by your perfidy—and though
I cannot approve of divorce, I find myself unable to
condemn your unfortunate husband to a contract so
inimical to his best interests. Consequently, the
marriage between you is dissolved, the divorce granted.
I am, I might add, in hope that you, young woman, will
learn the error of your ways. Given your previous
conduct, however, I wonder if that is possible." He
glared at her. "Have I said something to stir your
risibilities, madam?"

Julie bit down the delighted smile that was currently
curling her lips. "N-no, your honor," she managed to
say, but the smile would not be suppressed. This man,
this wonderful man, had freed her from her prisoning
marriage and she was hard put not to throw her arms
around his neck and kiss him! At the thought of his
reaction to such a gesture, her smile expanded to a grin.

The slap came long after the smile had vanished from
Julie's face. It was delivered three days later by her
mother, who had been informed of her reaction in the
judicial chamber by her shocked and horrified brother.
For one so frail and ill, a mere wraith—the lady's own
description of herself—she had managed to inflict
considerable pain on her daughter's cheek and the
corner of her mouth. Ignoring Sir Henry's protests, the
invalid launched into a diatribe which, in addition to
invoking heaven's curse upon the head of her erring
daughter, also prophesied a long life and a lonely one
as, shunned by all society, she eked out her miserable
existence in the confines of Carleton Manor.

Julie, her own anger surpassing that of the parent
who was, in her estimation, responsible for all that had
befallen her, by refusing to heed her weeping remon-
strances that she could not like Sir Edwin, turned an icy
glance upon her mother's face, saying clearly, "I prefer

being lonely and in disgrace, Mama. Indeed, I had much rather be dead than married to Edwin."

"It is a great pity that you did not die," retorted her ladyship, sinking wearily back on her pile of pillows. "Certainly to all intents and purposes, you are as good as dead. And—"

"That is quite enough, Viola!" Sir Henry, a silent and uncomfortable observer of this scene, put his arm around Julie's shoulders. "There is no need to rub more salt in our daughter's wounds."

"*Your* daughter," his spouse said pointedly. "She is nothing to me. I refuse to recognize her existence. Henceforth, let her be excluded from my sight. Indeed, it were better that she be removed from this house and sent away. Certainly, while she remains here, we cannot receive our innocent grandchildren here and . . . Hold!" She glared at a retreating Julie. "Where are you going? I have not excused you from my presence as yet."

Julie said composedly. "Have you not, Mama? I had the distinct impression that you had. And whether you have or not, I think you must consider your indifferent health. Mr. Craig, I seem to remember, said that you were not to be overexcited." So saying, Julie moved quietly out of the room, closing the door softly behind her. Crossing the hall hastily, she dashed up the stairs to her own chamber and once more closed the door quietly. It was not until she was standing near the window that she dared to loose the laugh of sheer pleasure that, during the course of her mother's diatribe, she had had the greatest difficulty in suppressing.

Lady Viola's slap had been hurtful, but her words were not, and neither the blow nor the tongue-lashing could erase her great relief at being divorced and disgraced! Her condition was, after all, hardly different from what it had been before she had been so summarily forced to wed Sir Edwin Fitzroy. Her marriage had lasted no more than two months, and in the two hundred and five months of her previous existence, she had often been alone.

Christine, her youngest sister, had already passed her eleventh birthday when Julie was born, and by the time she was six, Christine was married to Sir Thomas Lambert, the son of another old friend of Lady Viola's. Seemingly, Christine, or Chrissie, as the family called her, was happy in her marriage, as was Eliza, the oldest girl. Julie's brothers, Raymond and Bernard, had also appeared similarly content, possibly, she reasoned, because Lady Viola had not been so eager to rid herself of her four older children. If she had thought about it, Julia decided indignantly, her mother must have guessed that she and Sir Edwin were not suited. He had never been enthusiastic about wedding her. The smile that had greeted her forced response to his proposal had not reached his eyes.

In fact, Julie thought contemptuously, he had to be a poor stick indeed to have bound himself to one for whom he appeared to have no feeling at all. In the miserable two months of their wedded life, she had scarcely seen him. At her husband's earnest request, Sir Mark had accompanied her to most of the functions to which she and Edwin were invited.

Julie winced. She had believed that Sir Mark, at least, was her friend. That she had been mistaken was only too obvious. A friend would not have plied her with champagne until she was so tipsy she hardly knew what was happening. Worse than that, he would not have left her alone in the box for such a long time.

She ran her hands through her thick blond hair, pulling at it as was her wont when deep in thought. Still, it did no good to sink deep in thought at this juncture! No matter how hard she racked her brains, she could not understand why Sir Mark had disappeared, and she could remember only vaguely Sir James's arrival in her box. She recalled being interested in the dancers on the floor and having a drink pressed into her hand that, when she had quaffed it, tasted entirely different from champagne. She could not remember having left the ball with him, nor could she remember arriving at his lodgings. She could remember waking in his bed the following morning.

He had been standing over her, wrapped in a most colorful dressing gown. She could also remember his saying, "Well, well, my little sleeping beauty . . . how are you this morning?"

She had replied that she had a pounding headache, and then, belatedly, she had sat up, dragging the covers around herself—her bare self! She had been completely unclad! In a panic, she had asked him why she was there and he had answered with a horrid self-satisfied smile that she must be teasing him that she could not remember the heady excitement of the previous night— their rapturous night of love, as he had dubbed it.

"You were a most willing partner," he had told her.

Had she been? She must have been extremely foxed . . . and even so, it did seem odd that she would have *wanted* him to make love to her. Ever since that horrid night with Edwin, she had shrunk from the very idea of "love." She could not imagine herself responding to Sir James's advances—even if she were foxed. The very idea was entirely loathsome. And if she were as inebriated as he had suggested, how could she have responded at all? It was extremely confusing—but actually, that night had served its purpose. She was divorced, divorced, divorced! She need never see Edwin Fitzroy again, and she had not to bear his horrid name either. She could be plain Julie Carleton and she would be left in peace, perfect peace for the rest of her life!

"Oh," Julie murmured happily as she turned away from the window, "it is truly delightful to be divorced and disgraced."

1

Clad in the black gown the village seamstress had run up hastily, Julie Carleton stood in her father's huge chamber, where his body was laid out on the massive bed. Mrs. Ames, the housekeeper, had been with her recently. Between muffled sobs she had said, "Oh, if 'e don't look like 'e were asleep, Miss Julie."

He did not look as if he were asleep. Julie had sat with him night and day for the last three weeks. The change had been immediate and had come with his last breath, the breath after the one in which he had bidden her farewell. Tears stood in her eyes and were blinked away.

When he had still been able to speak, he had said, "I beg that you will not weep for me, dearest Julie. It has been a good life and I have had you at my side. I thank God for that mercy. And I beg you, do not change our plans in any way. You will find that I have made provision for you in my will, and I insist that you do as we had intended to do—together, before the onslaught of this illness. You must promise me that you will honor this, my last wish."

"Oh, Father," she had whispered. "How can I?"

"Julie . . ." He had half-risen. "You must. I will not have you here with your brother's family—forever holding you in opprobrium for something we both know was no fault of yours. You will do exactly as we

15

planned, else I swear I will come back and haunt you! So give me your promise, Julie.''

"I . . . I promise, Father," she had said.

The sick man's face had lighted. "There's my good girl, my very good girl. You have made these last years very happy, you know."

"And you have made me very happy, Father. Oh, dear, what will I do without you?"

His eyes had brightened. "I am of the opinion that you will do very well indeed, my dearest child— especially with such remarkable talents as you possess. And I do thank God for these last six years. They have been quite the happiest of my life."

"You know how much they have meant to me, Father."

"Ah." He had managed to raise his hand to touch her cheek. "You deserve more, my love, and will have more. And I charge you once again. I cannot, I think, say this too often. Do not let your brothers and sisters intimidate you. They will try as one or another of them has tried for the last eight years, but I beg you will not heed them. That is another promise you must give me."

"You have it, Papa," she had said firmly.

She looked at the bed and then looked away, preferring the image in her mind's eye. "Yes, you have it, Papa," she whispered, and emerging from his room, she hurried down the stairs.

The family was expected imminently. There would be eight adults and there might be children, as well, if one could designate a niece and a nephew two and three years her senior as children. They were the offspring of her brother Raymond. She doubted that Eliza would bring Evelina, Andrew, and Peregrine—even though at nineteen, seventeen, and fourteen, they could hardly be corrupted by the presence of their erring aunt. Bernard's five children would, of course, not be present. He, following in the footsteps of a maternal uncle, had become a clergyman. He had a very good living in Bristol and it would not do if one of the five were to acquaint a parishioner with the tale of his erring sister Julie. Even though eight years had come and gone, the parish gossips could make it seem as if the whole sorry situation had taken place only yesterday! Bernard, Julie thought wryly, would be very glad she was leaving. He had not made an appearance at the Manor since their mother's death six years back.

"Poor Mama was brought to her final resting place by your erring ways," he had intoned as they returned from the funeral.

"Stuff and nonsense," his father had growled. "Viola was ailing these twenty years and more. 'Twas a quinsy took her off."

"Ah, Father, you are truly forgiving," Bernard had sighed. His wife had sighed too, and darted a quelling look at Julie.

They would be sighing in unison today, Julie thought, and hastily downed a smile. It was not a time for smiling. Still, despite the very real grief she felt for her father's passing, she would be hard put not to show her amusement at her family's combined effort not to treat her like a pariah on this, the saddest of all occasions. Undoubtedly their efforts would last no longer than the end of the funeral. Subsequently there would be conferences on that all-important topic: "What shall we do with Julie?"

Raymond, heir to the title and the estate, would be called upon to preside over those semisecret meetings. Julie smiled wryly, using her mind's eye once more to envision the arguments and, possibly, the quarrels that must needs arise as they attempted to find a solution to this most unpleasant problem.

And then Mr. Soames, the family lawyer, would appear, will in hand.

"I will see that you are independent, Julie."

She started and glanced over her shoulder. Had she really heard her father's voice? Of course she had not. It was a memory, a memory of his promise, followed by her own to abide by the plans they had made before he had been stricken by what had proved to be a mortal illness.

"And I will, Papa, I promise," she whispered to the image in her mind's eye.

"Miss Julie," Price, the elderly butler said, as he met her in the hall, "there's been word from the gates. Mr. Raymond . . . Sir Raymond has arrived."

"Very well, Price. Show him . . ." She paused, struck by the notion that directly her brother entered the great hall, she would no longer be giving orders to the servants. "I will go to greet him," she amended.

"Yes, Miss Julia," the butler said. There was, she noted, a trace of regret in his tone, and she guessed that he might be anticipating some manner of unpleasantness. There would be none, she decided. Or, if there were, it would not be of her creating. She would do her best to remain impervious to the slurs that would undoubtedly come her way.

Though Raymond was the first to arrive, the others came almost on his heels, and several times in the course of greeting them, Julie was forced to remember her decision. It took considerable strength of will to abide by it—as she met censorious gaze after censorious gaze and, subsequently, the combined efforts of her siblings and in-laws to put her in her "rightful place," as it were. She was well aware that they were retaliating for the six years when she had, at her father's express desire, acted as his hostess. There was to be no more of that, as Lady Alicia, Raymond's wife, had obviously concluded.

When Julie, momentarily forgetting her change in status, had said, "I have put you in the Yellow Room,

Raymond," Alicia had cut in to say icily, "We would prefer the Green chamber."

"I had assigned that to—"

"I think, dearest Julie," Lady Alicia had interrupted with one of her pseudo-sweet smiles, "that you had best leave the assigning of the chambers to us."

"Very well, Alicia, but the Yellow Room has the morning sun and the Green Room is rather dark—but certainly you have the right to reapportion them. I hope that I may remain in my chamber for the nonce—or do you already have plans for that?"

"Of course we do not, Julie," Raymond had said quickly, with a sharp glance at his wife. "Let Julie's choices remain for the time being, my dear."

He had received an angry glare from Lady Alicia, but she had yielded, though not without a sting in her speech. "Very well, Raymond, dear. I expect Julie does know the house better than all of us—who have not had the pleasure of visiting it as often as we might."

"But, my dear Alicia," Julie had been quite unable to keep from commenting, "its doors have always been open to you. Papa often remarked that he was sorry to see you so seldom."

"You . . . " Lady Alicia had seemed without words.

"Shall we go to our rooms, my dear?" Raymond had spoken pacifically, but his eyes, resting on his sister's face, were cold.

She had not expected and did not get better treatment from the rest of the family. Indeed, her own earlier prediction was more than borne out as the others arrived. More than once in the course of greeting them, Julie longed for her father's ameliorating presence. Indeed, as the butler ushered in the last of them, she could almost imagine Sir Henry at her side, his eyes bright with derision as he practically compelled them to greet his erring daughter with a cordiality she did not deserve.

None of them had ever understood or approved his attitude. She had the definite feeling that they considered him in his dotage and themselves forced to be deferential until the time came when deference was no longer required. That time had finally come, and with it frozen stares on the part of her two sisters-in-law and embarrassment mirrored in the eyes of her brothers-in-law.

Eliza, as was her wont, still went out of her way to be kind to Julie—even though her kindness had more than a measure of condescension. Chrissie, on the other hand, was even colder than Lady Alicia. Julie did not resent her attitude. She had once heard her sister weepingly tell Sir Henry that her husband watched her every move and if she so much as smiled on a gentleman, he immediately brought up her sibling's disgrace.

Chrissie, who was quite the prettiest girl in the family, at least in Julie's estimation, was also the most flirtatious. Julie could well imagine that she fretted over her clipped wings. However, Chrissie's dislike had more than one root. Until Julie's birth, Chrissie had been the youngest child, and being so pretty, had received the lion's share of attention from her father. With the advent of Julie, she had been displaced in his affections, or so it had seemed to her. Furthermore, her dearest Mama had become ill and fretful, unable to stomach overlong the presence of eleven-year-old Chrissie. Consequently her resentment was threefold. That had been only too evident as she had come in on the arm of Sir Thomas Lambert, her husband. Sir Thomas was no more cordial. He had definitely been on the side of those relations who insisted that Julie be sent to the country—a vague term for far, far away, where the scandal could be decently buried along with its

perpetrator. Judging from the chill that had emanated
from him, he was still of that same opinion and was
eagerly contemplating that moment when the sentence
could be carried out by himself and his assorted connections.

Julie had a moment of wishing that Time's winged
sandals might be speeded up until the hour when she
could free herself from the weighty presence of her
family. Time obliged some two hours later. Finally,
when they were all in their rooms either preparing
themselves for that moment when they would be paying
their last respects to the late Sir Henry or resting from
the exigencies attendant upon so long a journey, Julie
slipped out of the house and into the gardens.

Spring had arrived early this year and now, at the end
of April, the flowers were looking lovely. The sight of
them pleased and soothed her. The yellow daffodils
were always so cheerful, and the tulips, in purple, white,
and yellow, were also much to her taste. Her father had
loved flowers, and each day of his illness she had
brought him a large bouquet of them. She sighed,
wishing that he were with her at this moment enjoying
the bounties of spring. Wishing, alas, would not bring
him back. She shivered slightly, wondering what lay
ahead for her. The combined disdain of her family had
not been as easy to shrug away, now that her father was
no longer present to intercede for her. She wondered if
he had ever acquainted any of them with his theories
concerning her divorce. And would her relations have
credited them, if he had?

She had a feeling that they would not. It was easier to
imagine her a villainess rather than a victim. *Had* she
been a victim? She ran her hands through her heavy
hair, a habit when she was thinking. Unwillingly she
cast her mind back to the night of the masquerade. Had
Edwin been unnaturally eager for her to go?

Yes, he had!

He, who had seemed entirely indifferent to her needs, had insisted that she and Sir Mark go—the sooner, the better. However, she had not really needed any persuasion. She had been quite eager to see a spectacle Sir Mark had described in detail, and he had already proved himself to be a very pleasant companion. She did remember being surprised that he had left their box so early and had remained away such a long time—long enough so that Sir James could say later that he had thought her alone in the box, adding that he had never seen her escort. Sir James, who had sounded the death knell of her marriage. Her father had, at first, vociferously blamed her for having encouraged him. However, that anger had turned to suspicion when Sir Edwin, immediately the divorce was granted, had demanded that he keep Julie's dowry—to "assuage the wounds inflicted on my heart" had been his words.

Her mother had insisted that "poor, cuckolded Sir Edwin" be allowed to keep it. "Certainly your daughter will have no use for it in the future," she had said coldly. "She has no future." She had also waxed loud and long upon the pain Julie had inflicted upon Lady Fitzroy, her very best friend.

Julie winced. Her mother had ceased speaking to her after she returned home. If she had need to address her, her directions were given either to a servant or to Sir Henry. Lady Viola had looked straight through her as if she were not there. She had also insisted that Julie take her meals in the old nursery. There had been many arguments about that attitude, she knew. There had also been arguments concerning Sir Henry's kindness to one who deserved nothing more than total ostracism.

Then, exactly one month to the day after the divorce, Sir Edwin had married again—Sir Markham's sister Mary. Sir Mark had been his best man. Prominent among the wedding guests had been Sir James Massinger. The quarrel that this news engendered proved loud and long, with Lady Viola stubbornly citing the fact that Sir Edwin's hasty marriage was a balm to his wounded ego and Sir Henry saying that it was his opinion that their unfortunate daughter had been trapped and traduced—and why could not her mother see that?

Lady Viola had not been able to see the maneuvers that had resulted in Sir Edwin's becoming considerably richer than he had been before receiving Julie's substantial dowry. She had suggested that her husband must be in his dotage for advancing such a theory. Julie smiled grimly. Her mother had obviously wanted her to be in the wrong. It was more than possible that she had long sought a reason on which to base the dislike in which she had held her daughter since her birth. Having found it, she was determined not to discard it. Julie had remained in Coventry until the day of her mother's death, when, sitting at Lady Viola's bedside, out of duty rather than inclination, she had finally heard her name on the lips of her expiring parent.

"You . . . have . . . driven . . . me to . . . an early grave," had been the effortful whisper.

"Nonsense, Viola," Sir Henry, sitting on the opposite side of the bed, had snapped. "You have lived far beyond your doctor's expectations. You are sixty-one. My own mother died at forty-nine." The fact that his wife had expired in the midst of delivering an angry rebuttal had not appeared to disturb him. He had only been upset at the possible effect of her last words upon Julie. He had earnestly begged her to forget them.

She had not needed his prompting. She had never liked her mother and, at present, she was hard put to remember what she looked like—save that the portrait in the gallery was more flattering than she deserved.

That, of course, might not be true, she amended mentally. She had never seen her mother as a young woman. However, it was her father's contention that both Eliza and Raymond resembled her, and while they were well-looking, neither had any claims to great beauty. And why, she wondered, was she dwelling on her mother, who, having finally acquired a reason to hate her, had done so with unceasing vigor?

"Were I ever to have children . . ." she whispered, and then smiled derisively. That was unlikely—since no one would ever marry her. Her lost reputation must needs preclude that. And furthermore, she had absolutely no desire ever to marry again. There were times even now when she remembered her wedding night and the pain inflicted by her husband's merciless invasion.

"And who might you be, my lovely?" inquired a most interested male voice.

Julie turned swiftly and looked up to find a tall young man of some twenty-seven or -eight years, she guessed, coming toward her. He was dressed to the nines in a well-fitting black coat over white unmentionables. The tassels on his gleaming Hessian boots were a bright gold and he was wearing a tall beaver hat. A many-caped coat hung over his shoulders and he was in the process of pulling off driving gloves. His face, she realized, seemed vaguely familiar, though she was hard put to place it. Was he a cousin or . . . ? Before she could dwell any further on his identity, he had reached her side and slipped an arm around her waist, saying in appreciative tones, "I did not expect to find such a one among my female relations. Whose daughter might you be, my beautiful? But no matter, you cannot object to a cousinly kiss?"

"I . . . am not your cousin, sir," she cried. "I—"

"All the better, though I have scarce seen an abigail

so easy on the eyes. My late grandfather is to be con-
gratulated!''

"Sir, please—" she began, and was silenced by a
long, invading kiss.

Immediately he raised his head, there was a long
shriek above them as, from a window, Chrissie cried,
"You vile creature! Would you be adding incest to your
other crimes?" The window was slammed shut at the
same time that Julie managed to free herself from the
young man.

She glared up at him, running a hand across her
mouth. "How c-could you?" she demanded hotly.
"And who . . . who are you?"

He had been directing a glance toward the window,
but now he faced her, a flush on his cheeks. "Who are
you?"

"I am Julia Carleton," she responded freezingly.

He took a step back, looking thunderstruck. "By
God, you . . . you'll not be telling me that!"

"I asked you a question, sir," Julie said sharply, her
heart beginning to pound heavily in her chest and
seemingly in her throat as well.

"I am David Carleton, your nephew. I . . . I am
sorry. But no matter, I will tell that pack of . . . I will tell
them that it was my error. I thought, you see—"

"You have told me what you thought!" she snapped.
"You thought I was an abigail and, consequently,
unable to defend myself against your advances. And
possibly you imagined that one of my lowly stature
might even be grateful for the attentions of a so-called
gentleman?"

His flush deepened. "I . . . am afraid you are right.
But you see, you are so incredibly . . ." He paused as his
Aunt Chrissie, followed by his Uncle Thomas and his
mother came rushing across the grass. "Oh, Lord," he
muttered. "You—"

Before he could finish speaking, Sir Thomas, who was well in the lead, reached Julie. Clutching her by the shoulders, he shook her roughly. "You wanton . . ." he snarled. "The idea of . . . of . . . trying to seduce your own blood kin!"

David inserted himself between Julie and his uncle. "She seduced no one," he said sharply.

"My poor, poor David." Lady Alicia had reached her son's side. "How did she—?"

"Mother," he interposed hastily, "you . . . all of you are quite mistaken. I had no notion of this . . . young lady's identity when I . . . er, kissed her."

"Naturally, she would not tell you!" Chrissie cried.

"And whether he knew it or not, he is always gallant." Lady Alicia glared at Julie.

"I was not in the least gallant," David sighed.

"No," Julie snapped, "you certainly were not." She turned to Lady Alicia. "It seems that your son mistook me for an abigail!"

"Do not tell me that you did not invite his . . . his attentions!"

"She did not," David said earnestly. "I did think she was an abigail, and I agree with her: I should not have tried to take advantage of her. It is only that—"

"You need not excuse yourself to her, my love!" Lady Alicia exclaimed.

"No, indeed," Chrissie cried. "He was as clay in her hands. I know what I saw . . . her movements were deliberately provocative." She glared at Julie. "I saw you beckon to him."

"I did not—" Julie began.

"And I, too, saw it." Sir Thomas glared at Julie. "I witnessed the whole shameful episode and found it quite in line with what I have heard about this . . . this abandoned creature!"

"You are lying," David stated flatly.

"David!" Lady Alicia gasped. "You must beg your uncle's pardon, and at once."

"I will not beg his pardon," her son growled. "She did not attempt to seduce me, as you say. I saw her walking in the garden. No one had told me she was so young and beautiful! I did not dream that she could be my aunt, and I can also tell you that I wish she were not!"

"David!" Lady Alicia groaned. "You cannot know what you are saying. This . . . this woman brought shame and disgrace to our name and to our house."

"That is only too true," Sir Thomas averred. He fastened his cold gaze on Julie's face. "If your father had heeded me, you would have been sent away—and shall be as soon as proper arrangements can be made."

"Uncle Thomas!" David regarded him with an anger mixed with shock. "You will not speak to her in such terms in my presence or I shall be compelled to—"

"David!" Lady Alicia cried. "No more, if you please! You know not of what, or rather of whom, you speak!"

"To the contrary, Mother," he responded tartly, his cool gaze traveling over the angry faces of his kin. "I have heard of her so-called crime throughout the greater part of my life, and I tell you yet again, she was not to blame for this incident. It was my doing and mine alone."

"Oh," Julie sighed, "I beg you will cease your defense of me, my dear David. They are primed to neither hear nor credit anything you say on my behalf. As for myself, I do not care what they believe. I never have." So saying, she turned her back on them, and moving swiftly across the garden, reached the house and hurried inside. A few minutes later she had reached her own chamber. Closing and locking the door, she sank down on the bed. She was hard put to decide whether she was angry or amused at Chrissie's wild accusations and those of Sir Thomas. She decided that amusement was not the proper attitude for either. Chrissie must certainly have seen David take the initiative, and she was certain that Sir Thomas was equally aware of her efforts to free herself from the young man's constraining embrace.

She had a sudden conviction that they had been looking for trouble or, rather, hoping for it. Well, Raymond's lad had provided it, giving them both the opportunity to don the black caps of prosecuting judges. Then they had hurried with the tale to Alicia, who, in common with themselves, hated and resented Sir Henry's determined partisanship. No doubt they deemed him half-senile. And what would they say when they heard his will? It did not matter. They could do nothing.

She smiled suddenly. It occurred to her that rather than dreading it, she must needs look forward to that moment when they would hear her father's last will and testament. He had credited her with the advice that had, some two years earlier, earned him a very substantial sum of money. Since that time, he had discussed all his investments with her and had applauded her for a business sense which he deemed amazing in a female or, for that matter, anyone!

"You will not go unrewarded, my dearest Julie," he had gasped one night when, lying wakeful and in the grip of his final illness, he had found her sitting at his bedside. "You will be completely independent, my love."

No doubt he would leave her as much as five thousand pounds—since considerably more than that had been realized during the transactions.

How angry they would be, then—especially Sir Thomas and Chrissie. Five thousand pounds would enable her to live in comfort away from the Manor. She would not be sorry to leave her home, now that her father was dead. She had the odd feeling that the very heart of the house had gone with his last breath. A long sigh escaped her, and she blinked back a sudden wetness in her eyes. It was time to be practical, time to think of her future.

She would be able to afford at least two servants—Lucy, her abigail, and a cook. She would also keep a horse for riding or harnessing to the gig she planned to purchase. On the whole, she preferred to ride. She would live very quietly, no longer a thorn in the side of her family, and the lot of them would no longer be a whole set of thorns in her side. Given David's untoward actions, they would undoubtedly be glad to be rid of her. Sir Thomas had waxed warmly on her fate, she remembered. In fact, she reasoned, she ought not be annoyed with her nephew's precipitate behavior. On the contrary, she had every reason to be grateful to him. He had pounded the last nail in her so-called coffin, and she was free!

She rose and moved toward her armoire, glad that Lady Alicia had not responded to her sarcastic offer of her own chamber. It would have been extremely embarrassing to have moved out of it—especially since the armoire and her chests of drawers were almost bare of clothing. Her bandboxes had been packed early that morning, and only the gowns she would wear for the next three days remained. Once the lawyer had read the will, she would be out of the Manor and on her way to Brighton! Her family might raise objections—but she could not imagine that these would be more than mere lip service. Undoubtedly they would be only too delighted to see the last of her.

2

On the morning of the day the will was to be read, Julie, staring out of her window, watched the sun climbing toward its zenith. She had seen it rise and she had also seen it appear in the guise of a faint red streak along the eastern horizon. Now it was almost time for Mr. Soames to arrive. She smiled wryly. It was well he had elected to come on the day following the funeral. She did not believe she could bear another twenty-four hours of her family's determined disapproval, a condition that was combined with their concern over her ultimate destination—once she was ejected from a house she could no longer consider her home.

In the twenty-four hours since the funeral had briefly united them all in a common grief, Julie, passing from room to room, had been aware of sudden startled cessations of low-voiced discussions. These silences had been accompanied by indignant glances, as if, indeed, they suspected her of deliberate eavesdropping. However, one did not need to be an eavesdropper to guess the subject of those conversations. They were, of course, trying to determine how to dispose of her. Obviously they believed that it was the duty of one or another brother or sister to harbor her. That it was a burden none wished to assume was only too obvious.

Julie had the distinct feeling that Sir Thomas was in favor of sending her to some bastion deep in the country

with a housekeeper who would be a keeper in every
sense of the word. Ever since that episode in the garden,
he had regarded her with a deep disgust. Julie was, in
fact, positive that he believed she had invited her
nephew's unwanted attentions. Chrissie, of course, was
entirely willing to doubt the evidence of her own eyes,
and she, together with her husband, had made a victim
out of David and a villain out of Julie. Raymond, unfortunately, had been convinced of her complicity by
Lady Alicia, and Bernard was only too willing to agree.
He had cornered her yesterday and read her what
amounted to a sermon on her wickedness in seducing
the young. Everyone in the family seemed bent on forgetting that David was, in fact, three years her senior.

Indeed, judging from the way he was avoiding her,
David himself might be half-convinced that she had
sung the siren song that had brought him hot-footed to
her side—no, that was not true. David, at least, was
avoiding her out of embarrassment. His sister, Jane,
had told her that, adding that both of them were in-
furiated by the deliberate efforts of the family to heap
more blame on her head. Yet, grateful as she was for
their partisanship, she knew that she would have been in
sore straits indeed, were it not for her father's promise.
Humble pie was neither filling nor tasty, and left to the
kind offices of her family, she would have been dining
upon it for the rest of her life. A little laugh shook her—
her father had saved her from that horrid fate, at least!

Still, despite her certainty that Sir Henry would do as
he had promised, Julie, coming into the library for the
reading of the will, found herself nervous. There was a
possibility that he might have had second thoughts, and
fearing that she was not capable or competent enough to
handle a sum as large as five thousand pounds, provided
that he had left her that much, he might have decided
that she must have a guardian. He had been extremely

reticent regarding the sum he had promised to leave her. He had contented himself with saying only, "You will find it adequate to your needs—throughout your life, my love."

Five thousand pounds invested wisely would certainly be adequate for her needs. And she knew about investing. Mr. Soames was in agreement on that count. In common with her father, he had praised her acumen, calling it remarkable for a female. In fact, he had gone as far as to say that it was remarkable for anyone, man or woman, especially one unversed in such matters until she had begun to read the financial reports sent to her father. Consequently she was wrong to harbor the doubts currently plaguing her. She blamed them on the atmosphere of censure and blame that had persisted ever since the episode in the garden.

Finally the lawyer and the hour of the reading had arrived. Julie, taking her seat some little distance from her assembled family, was even more aware of their combined disapproval and dismay. Though nothing was said, the question of what was to be done with Julie was obviously uppermost in their minds. Only David and his sister had kind looks for her, and, of course, Mr. Enoch Soames, the lawyer, was cordial.

Her thoughts fled, for the reading had commenced. The servants were remembered first, and then Raymond received a large bequest. There were smaller bequests for Bernard, Eliza, and Chrissie, and then there were the words, sonorously, almost pontifically read by Mr. Soames: " . . . and lastly, to my beloved daughter Julie I give and bequeath the sum of fifty thousand pounds."

Julie's hand flew to her mouth, and for a moment there was absolute silence in the room. Then Sir Thomas rose to his feet crying, "But he must have been mad!"

The storm broke, crashing about Julie's ears as the assembled company all spoke at once. Then, again, Sir

Thomas' voice was louder than the rest. He planted himself in front of Julie. "You abandoned woman, what did you do to influence a childish old man?" he thundered.

"Sure, it was collusion . . . the will must be . . . must be overturned," Lady Alicia shrilled.

"But of course, it must be madness. Where did my father get fifty thousand pounds? And saying that he did have such a sum at his disposal, why would he leave it to that . . . that scarlet woman?" Bernard demanded.

"He could not possess that much. It was a fantasy arising from his illness. The truth of the matter is that Julie has been left nothing!" Chrissie exclaimed, not without some satisfaction at a hypothesis in which she obviously believed.

The lawyer waited patiently until the furor died down. Then he said, "You have not given me the opportunity to finish the reading of the will. May I please have your attention, ladies and gentlemen?"

"You have it," Sir Raymond snapped.

The lawyer cleared his throat. "The sum in question goes to my dear daughter for her invaluable advice in the deposition of my funds. It is her share. The rest, which amounts to seventy-five thousand pounds, will be held in trust for the children of her siblings, who have reason to be grateful to her for her intelligence. My daughter has not wasted her years in idle regret. She has been my great comfort and joy, and this is the least I could do for her. If any question is raised as to my sanity, you must confer with Mr. Enoch Soames, who will tell you that he and three colleagues, including a judge, have declared me to be in full possession of my senses. I have appointed Mr. Soames as my daughter Julie's trustee."

There was another brief silence before Sir Thomas said harshly, "It is madness. I pray you will not tell me that he was of sound mind! What does a female know about financial matters?''

"What, indeed?" Lady Alicia echoed.

"I must add my query to that," Sir Raymond said gravely. "I have never known my sister Julie to be an . . . er, woman of business."

"She can know nothing," Bernard said gravely. "I still insist that there has been some manner of collusion here. My father was old and ailing at the last, and my sister was alone with him, ostensibly nursing him, but—"

"Mr. Carleton!" the lawyer interrupted indignantly. "Miss Carleton has proved herself to be remarkably astute when it comes to finances. I myself have profited from her advice."

"Why was I told nothing of this? As my father's eldest son, surely I had the right to know his intentions," Sir Raymond said angrily.

"I am still of the opinion that he was senile," Sir Thomas growled. "And I think we must not stand idly by while this . . . this travesty . . . Hold! Where are you going, Julie?"

Julie, who had unobtrusively risen, was at the door. She said composedly, "I am going to my room. I must finish my packing. I am leaving for Brighton tomorrow morning."

"You . . . are . . . leaving for Brighton tomorrow morning?" Sir Thomas echoed. "You are *leaving* and your poor father not cold in his grave?"

With muted satisfaction Julie said, "I am obeying his wishes. We had planned on this journey before his illness, and he told me that I must go. It was his last wish."

"Nonsense." Sir Raymond rose to his feet. "You cannot go to Brighton. You are in mourning."

"Papa desired that I mourn him in Brighton," Julie retorted.

"No, no, no, we cannot countenance that, my dear. It is quite out of the question," Bernard said.

"Of course it is." Lady Alicia had also risen. "You must stay here with us, my dear Julie. Certainly you cannot leave at such a time. It . . . it is unheard-of."

"You can stay with William and myself, Julie dear," Eliza said. "William is chair-bound, as you know, but I am sure he would be delighted to see you again, and naturally, you must long for a change of scene. Somerset is beautiful at this time of year."

"No more beautiful than Bristol," Bernard snapped. "You must come to us, Julie."

"I do not wish to stay with anyone," Julie said evenly. "I am going to Brighton. As I have explained, it was Papa's earnest desire that I do so. And now, if you will excuse me, I must finish my packing." She hurried out of the room.

Her heart was pounding heavily as she hastened up the stairs. She was also chiding herself for having disclosed her plans. Naturally, they would be most reluctant to let her out of their sight—now that she was an heiress. Fifty thousand pounds! It was a vast sum, and even though she had, in a sense, earned it, they would be determined to keep it and her own person in the family—"away from fortune hunters" would be their excuse. An ironic little smile played about her lips. The undesirable Miss Julie Carleton had suddenly become the extremely desirable Miss Julie Carleton, and with a little thrill of fear she belatedly realized that they might actually contrive to keep her there.

Once in her room, she hastily rang for Lucy, and when the abigail appeared, she said, "I think we must leave even sooner than I had anticipated. Could you be ready at dawn on the morrow?"

"Oh, yes, Miss Julie." Lucy nodded.

There was a tap on her door. As the girl started toward it, Julie caught her arm. "No," she whispered.

"Do not let anyone in!" She moved toward the door. "Who is it?" she called.

"It is I, Alicia. Let me in, Julie."

"I am sorry, but I am resting, Alicia. And I really do not believe we have anything to say to each other."

"To the contrary, Julie," came the crisp reply. "We have something to say to you. You are not going to Brighton. It would be scandalous to leave for a . . . a resort at such a time. Your brother Raymond will not permit it. We are quite sure that your father desired him to act as your guardian, and he will take on that duty—immediately."

"My father did not appoint a guardian for me," Julie said evenly. "And I will not accept Raymond in that capacity. I am of age and perfectly capable of making my own decisions. I am going to Brighton, Alicia."

"The family has decided that you must remain here where you will be safe, Julie."

"Oh, Miss Julie," Lucy muttered, turning a frightened face toward her.

Though Julie was also beginning to be fearful, she still said calmly, "I do not feel safe here and I will do as I choose. I am leaving tomorrow."

"Raymond has countermanded the orders you sent to the stables. You are to go nowhere."

Julie pulled open her door. "Are you suggesting that I am your prisoner?" she demanded angrily.

Lady Alicia said icily, "Anything that we decide is for your own good. You do not know the ways of the world, Julie."

"I thought that the family believed quite the opposite," Julie said caustically. Her hands were knotted into fists, fists that she longed to shove into her sister-in-law's eyes.

"I am not going to argue with you." Lady Alicia's tone had reached the freezing mark. "I came only to give you our decision."

"You have no right, none of you," Julie cried, her fury overcoming her discretion.

"We have every right to protect your good name."

"I do not have a good name, as you well know, Alicia. I am divorced and disgraced," Julie retorted.

"That is all the more reason why you require our protection. You have already shown yourself to be foolish and wanting in discretion. And now . . . with such an immense sum at your disposal . . . there's no telling what might happen were you left to your own devices."

"I am not seventeen any longer. I am—"

"I beg you will cease to argue. It will avail you nothing. As I have explained, I came only to give you our decision. I had best leave you now." There was such overweening self-satisfaction in Lady Alicia's tone that Julie quite longed to slap the sister-in-law she had always hated, but that would have done her no good. Resisting an impulse to slam her door, she closed it quietly, and turning to Lucy, she said, "I expect you heard that."

"Oh, yes, Miss Julie." Lucy looked distressed. "I do think it 'igh-'anded o' them, I do. Not showin' their faces 'ere from one year to the next'n now—"

"Precisely." Julie took a turn around the room. "I never should have mentioned Brighton, I knew that the minute I said it. It was most foolish, but I was not thinking clearly and . . ." She paused. "What's that?" she whispered.

"Wot's wot?" Lucy looked surprised.

"I heard . . ." Julie paused, listening.

"I do not 'ear—"

"Shhhhh." Julie put a finger to her lips and was silent a moment. "There," she said. "At the window, a . . . a tapping."

"At the window, Miss Julie, 'ow could that be?" Lucy asked fearfully. "Oh, miss, you dasn't open it," she hissed as Julie made her way toward the tall windows. "Per'aps 'tis the ghost o' . . . ." She spoke to the air as Julie, thrusting open one side of the casement windows facing the gardens, stared out. A low whistle alerted her to David laying below her on one of the sturdy branches of the oak tree growing outside that same window.

"David . . ." she murmured.

"My dear"—he was panting slightly—"are you game to come out this way? It is a very sturdy tree."

"I . . . What are you telling me?" Julie asked.

"I am telling you that Mr. Soames's coach is a few paces up the road. I have spoken to him and we are agreed that you must get away as soon as possible. He will take you to Brighton, you and your abigail. It remains only for you to climb down this tree. It is not nearly dark enough—but the sun is setting, and if they should note your absence, you will have a head start. Are you game?"

"Oh, I am . . . I am," she whispered excitedly. "I have climbed down that tree many times . . . or at least I did when I was little. They wish to imprison me, do they not?"

He visited a shamed, regretful look on her face. "Yes, they do. They intend to keep you under lock and key and will give you no peace until you agree to entrust my . . . my father with your capital. He has appointed himself your guardian . . ." He sighed. "It is no more than plain robbery. I never thought to see my own father a party to so sorry a scheme—my mother too. My sister and I . . . " He shook his head. Then, before she could comment, he added, "We must waste no time. I expect you are already packed."

"Yes." Julie nodded. "I am taking very little. Papa told me that there are excellent mantau-makers in Brighton, and also one can buy ready-made garments

there. I have enough money to last me for the time
being."

"And also you will have Mr. Soames, who, as your
trustee, will provide you with more. I think you must go
as soon as possible—they are deep in discussion now—
or, rather, an argument—and I have an idea it will be
some time before they have reached a decision."

"Let us go, then," Julie said decisively. She glanced
over her shoulder and found Lucy behind her. "I hope
you will not mind using this window," she said.

"Oh, no, Miss Julie'n I think we'd best 'urry."

"Good," David said. "I suggest you throw your
bandboxes down first."

The tree had spreading branches, and Julie, despite a
slight nervousness, found that her prowess at climbing
had lost nothing in the intervening years. She moved
nimbly, if cautiously, from branch to branch, and
David, who had reached the ground first, lifted her
down. He performed the same service for an equally
agile Lucy, and retrieving the bandboxes, he said softly,
"It there a way out that skirts the gatekeeper's
cottage?"

"There is," Julie told him. "There's a break in one of
the hedges fronting the road."

"Oh, yes, so there be." Lucy giggled. "I know
it."

"Then we must use it. We will be meeting Mr.
Soames by that little copse near the stream. He will be
just over the bridge. I charge you that since it is still
light, let us move from tree to tree—and be careful
where you step, lest it be on a dry branch."

"Oh, we will," Julie murmured.

"And," David added, "I think you'd best let me
carry your bandboxes."

"Oh, I can do that, sir," Lucy whispered.

"No, you will have quite enough to do in getting

across the grounds to that hedge. I am sure you must agree."

"Well, per'aps yer right. An' I thank you, sir." Lucy sketched a curtsy and gratefully put the two bandboxes into his hands.

The way through the grounds was winding, and since it was still light, Julie, moving from tree to tree with Lucy and David close behind her, expected that at any moment they must meet a gardener or, perhaps, a keeper coming in from the adjacent woods. Yet, that would hardly matter . . . No, it might very well matter, if on stopping to speak to her they saw the bandboxes and noted that both she and Lucy were wearing bonnets and cloaks. She could not trust all who worked on the grounds. There were some who might be eager to curry favor with the new master and might hurry to spread the alarm. She could not dwell on that. She must keep walking, and . . . She bit down a little cry of joy; there was the hedge, and there, too, the large gap, right where she had thought it must be!

In a matter of seconds the three of them had edged through it, emerging onto a part of the road that was in a direct line with the gates—but the gatekeeper's cottage was behind the gates and set back several yards. The copse was to their left and not far distant. They rushed over the bridge and in another second they sighted the post chaise standing amidst the trees. A groom was soothing a team of four restive horses, and as Julie reached the door of the vehicle, it was hastily opened and the lawyer was smiling down at her.

"My poor child," he said. "I am sorry for this . . . But enough, get in and let us be away."

"I do thank you, sir." She turned to Lucy. "You get in. I wish to exchange one more word with David." She looked up at the lawyer. "I hope that is allowed, sir?"

"It is," he assented, "but let it be a very brief word,

my dear. We'll need to go a different route from the one I took in coming here . . . and there might be difficulty in finding it. Also, we must not rule out pursuit. I will not say that your family will guess you have gone with me . . ."

"I do understand," she assured him. "I will be brief." She hurried to David, who had just handed the bandboxes to the postboys. "I am much in your debt, my dear," she said gratefully.

He reached for her hands, and holding them warmly, he said, "No, it is I who must be in your debt, my dear Aunt Julie. I wish you Godspeed, and beg that you will forgive me for my part in your present woes."

"Of course I forgive you. I have forgotten all about it and, again, I do thank you."

"Let me thank you." He released her hands, and bowing, continued, "I will tell you something else, my dear. I could wish that you were not my aunt."

"Alas, that wish cannot be granted." She smiled up at him. "And furthermore, I must tell you that you have made me very glad that you are my nephew."

"My dear . . ." Mr. Soames called softly.

Julia, standing on tiptoe, brushed David's cheek with her lips. "Good-bye, my dear, and again, I thank you with all my heart." She hurried to the coach and was helped inside by another postboy. As the coachman flicked the reins and started off, Julie looked out of the window. David was still standing there staring after them. She waved again, but he did not wave back. Then the post chaise turned a bend in the road and he was lost to sight, he, the Manor, and all her other relatives, and if she chose, she thought happily, she need never see any of them again!

The trip to Brighton took three days, traveling at a good speed, and of course it was much out of Mr.

Soames's way, for which Julie apologized more than once. Indeed, the lawyer finally requested her to cease those apologies.

"My dear," he said gently, "you have suffered enough at the hands of your family. I was only too happy to rescue you from their clutches. And I can only say that I am shocked by their greed—especially since they were all very well remembered in the will. Still, I must admit that your father did entertain doubts as to their reception of the information I provided. I am glad that young David alerted me to their plans. Even though I had no inkling of them, I was yet racking my brains as to how I might intercede for you—should a contretemps of this nature arise."

"Oh, you are kind," she said gratefully.

He visited an odd look on her face. "You will find that I am not the only one who will be disposed to show you kindness, my dear Julie. Mine is, as I think I need not assure you, of a disinterested nature. However, I warn you, beware of . . . what you might term kindness when it is offered by those whom you do not know well. Indeed, were my dear wife not a semi-invalid, I would insist that she come to Brighton to chaperone you."

Julie gave him a reassuring smile. "I beg you will not concern yourself over me, sir. Not only am I of age, but I am also divorced and disgraced—a circumstance of which most of the *ton* is aware."

He laughed, but sobered immediately. "I promise you that word of your misdemeanor, if such it can be termed, will not be common knowledge now."

"It was common enough when it took place," Julie said. "I cannot count the number of people who appeared to take the greatest pleasure in cutting me dead."

"That was eight years ago, my dear, and since then a multitude of scandals have buried it deep in the sands of time. Still, you will be in mourning, and that, I think, should help hold the hounds at bay."

"Papa particularly requested me to abandon my mourning once I arrived in Brighton. He said he did not want to think of me in black."

The lawyer was silent for a moment. Then he said with a slight frown, "I think it were well that you did not abide by that particular request. The mourning will provide you some little protection against . . . well, kindnesses."

"I am not sure I understand you," she said confusedly.

"My dear, surely you cannot be unaware that you are"—he paused—"not unattractive."

Julie looked surprised. "I have never been complimented on my looks. Papa did say I was well-looking— but Mama did not agree, and neither did Edwin." She shuddered slightly.

"You have not seen your husband for years, nor your mother either. Speaking quite impartially, I would say that your appearance is most beguiling, and I beg you will be careful. You ought not to be alone here in Brighton. Indeed, I am more than half-inclined to ask my wife if she knows anyone she might recommend as a chaperone."

"I pray that you will not concern yourself, sir," Julie responded earnestly. "I am sure there will be at least one person here who will know me by reputation and spread the word."

"I do not wish to think of your suffering under an ancient disgrace, my dear," the lawyer said thoughtfully. "However, in this instance, I hope that you are right. Fortunately, no one knows about your inheritance, or you would be in the basket!"

Julie laughed. "I shall make it my main purpose in life to stay out of baskets, my dear Mr. Soames."

At their parting in the lobby of the Old Ship Hotel, where Julie would remain until she found a cottage to her liking, the lawyer had considerably more to say concerning her appearance, and again he stressed that she retain her mourning. "If your father were present, I am sure he would proffer the same advice," he told her earnestly.

Julie chuckled. "Were my father present, Mr. Soames, I should not be wearing mourning at all."

Mr. Soames also laughed, but sobered quickly. "Mark my words, my dear. And I beg of you—go nowhere without your abigail in attendance."

"Oh, I may safely promise that," Julie assured him.

It was with many misgivings, and the certain knowledge that Julie would, despite his advice, doff her black attire once she found a mantua-maker to supply her with new garments, that Mr. Soames left her.

On reaching London, he voiced his misgivings to a wife already exercised because of his failure to return as early as she had anticipated. Looking at him narrowly, she said coldly, "I am glad that you are back in London, Mr. Soames. It was kind of you to go out of your way for the chit, but I am sure that memories are longer than you imagine and that in a town such as Brighton, where the quality all know each other, the word will spread fast enough for her to need no other chaperone than my Lady Gossip."

There was something in her manner that caused Mr. Soames's expressions of concern to die aborning—but his worries did not desert him, and in the night, his unfettered consciousness sent a host of disturbing dreams which brought confusion in the morning and a tart suggestion from his wife that all his tossings and turnings suggested that he must be feverish. She attributed that to the chill air of Brighton and prepared a cordial which tasted extremely bitter. Still, feeling that he deserved it, the lawyer manfully swallowed it and prayed that he might exorcise the lovely image of Julie from his mind.

3

O nce they were settled, Julie said excitedly, "My first visit will be to a mantau-maker, Lucy. I do want to purchase some pretty new clothes."

Much to Julie's surprise and indignation, the abigail pronounced herself in agreement with Mr. Soames. "You ought to keep wearin' black, Miss Julie, an' 'twould be well if you was believed to be a widow. Besides, black is most becomin' to one o' your colorin'."

"I promised Papa that I would not wear black," Julie said firmly. "Now, let us go to the shops."

To do Julie justice, she made an effort to appease Lucy and the absent Mr. Soames by choosing a dimity gown of a pale lavender which, in her estimation, made her look quite washed-out. She also bought a gray silk for church, and rather than the bright blue shawl that attracted her, she purchased one in white.

"I cannot think," she said to a disapproving Lucy, "that anyone could fault these choices. After all, lavender and white *are* mourning colors, and gray is too."

"They would be mourning colors only if it were a year after your papa's death," Lucy grumbled. "Black would be better, Miss Julie. Then there'd not be anyone'd dare approach you."

"Lucy, they will not approach me," Julie explained

with a patience she was far from feeling. "Not only am I twenty-five years old and no longer young—I am divorced and disgraced." Unconsciously echoing Mrs. Soames, she added, "And in a small town such as Brighton, the news will spread quickly, you will see."

She did not understand her handmaiden's dour response: "That be just wot worries me, Miss Julie."

Julie refused to be concerned by Lucy's cavils. In fact, she could not understand them. During the eight years that had passed since her divorce, she had had considerable evidence of her fall from grace. On going to church with her father, she had been pointedly ignored by old friends of her parents' and by her own friends as well. When these married and moved away, she was cut by perfect strangers, who obviously knew of her disgrace.

She doubted that her experiences in Brighton would differ greatly from these. The world of the *ton* was small and stoked by gossip. Though, as yet, she had seen no familiar face when she and her abigail visited the mantau-maker or wandered through the parks, she was sure that one or another friend of her family would appear to point a finger and spread the word. She did not care. Once she found a house to her liking, she intended to purchase it and live out her days here.

These plans were in the future. During her initial month in the town, she intended to rest and enjoy the sea. She had a fine view of it from the window of her hotel room, but while she loved to gaze at it, her main objective was to go swimming. She had had a bathing dress made, and fully intended to wear it, the day after the final fitting. Unfortunately, Lucy had become ill the night before that proposed excursion. Even more unfortunately, she was still abed and fretful the following morning, attributing her malady to something she had eaten. Julie, while uttering words of comfort and making light of her own disappointment, found herself utterly beguiled by a brilliant sun and a gleaming sea. Having ascertained that the abigail had fallen asleep, she stealthily left the rooms and in a few moments was on her way, bathing dress in a bag that hung from her arm and which also contained her reticule. Her destination was the bathing machines, not too far distant, but she did not intend to remain there much above a half-hour. Lucy might never even know that she had gone.

The weather was even more beautiful than it had appeared from her window, and Julie felt particularly at peace with the world. In essence her father strode beside her, enjoying the salt-laden air and the gentle winds that ruffled her hair, newly cut and, in Lucy's estimation, extremely becoming. Filling Julie's eyes was the Marine Pavilion, now in the final stages of a metamorphosis that was turning it from an ordinary edifice into a Chinese Palace. Gazing at its bulging outlines, she laughed aloud, thinking that it must have appealed strongly to Sir Henry's well-developed sense of the ridiculous. In that same moment, she felt her arm seized, as an insinuating voice murmured, "Janet, as I live! I did not dream I should encounter you in Brighton. Well met, my love!"

Raising startled eyes, Julie blinked at a young man whose sartorial splendor surpassed even that of her nephew David. He was wearing a bright blue coat, a brocade waistcoat, a most intricately tied cravat, and ballooning trousers which, she knew, were called cossacks. He seemed, indeed, the very epitome of the London dandy. However, the voice in which he had addressed her was as coarse as his features, and she could not approve the appreciative gleam in his eyes or the insinuating smile that curved his full mouth. She said coldly, "I do not believe we have met, sir."

His smile broadened. "Could I have been mistaken? You are not Janet Beamish? Well"—he actually winked at her—"that is my misfortune, my dear. But then, perhaps, it is not. I will introduce myself. My name is Ronald Travers. And your name, my pretty?"

"I think that my name can be of little interest to you, sir. And I beg that you will please release my arm."

His grip actually tightened. "To the contrary, your name is of the greatest interest to me, my lovely one."

Julie tried to pull away. "I must ask you to let me go, if you please. I am on my way to meet my husband and—"

"Your husband? A fine husband to let a prime article like yourself walk out alone." He sneered. "Were I your husband, I would—"

"Sir," Julie interrupted angrily, "if you do not release me, I will scream."

"Ah, you have spirit! I admire spirit, my little lady-bird. Come, let us repair to yon tavern and—"

Her heart was beating heavily. "Let me go!" she said loudly enough to cause another man to turn around and stare at them. Heartened by his interest, she repeated, "I must ask you again to let me go. I do not know you."

"What is the matter here, pray?" The other man, equally well-dressed, though much less ostentatiously than her tormentor, stepped to her side. He continued coldly, "It seems that you are causing this young lady no little distress."

"I beg you'll not heed her. 'Tis a lovers' quarrel, no more," Mr. Travers growled.

"He is not my lover!" Julie cried indignantly. "I have never seen him before."

"Come, my little love," Mr. Travers said placatingly. "You'll be giving your knight-errant the wrong impression. I have said I am sorry. What more can I do?"

"You can go away!" Julie stamped her foot. "I am not your love. I am nothing to you!"

"I can believe that," the stranger agreed. "You are

out of your element, my good man. Your kind does not consort with ladies.''

"I am not your good man, damn you,'' Mr. Travers retorted furiously. "And if you do not let me see the back of you, very soon, I'll—'' Whatever else he might have said turned into a mumble as the other man's fist connected with his chin. He staggered back, his arms falling away from Julie. Then he lunged foward, only to be felled by another well-aimed blow. Rising shakily, he glared at his assailant. "Very well,'' he growled. "Have her. I wish you joy of the little wretch! She'll lead you a merry chase, she will.'' With another glare for Julie, he strode hastily away.

"I do thank you, sir,'' Julie said breathlessly. "I do hope you did not take any harm?''

"Not in the least,'' her rescuer assured her. "I could do no less, seeing you in such trouble.''

"I feared you might not believe me.'' She shuddered. "Imagine telling you that he and I—''

"How could I not believe you?'' he interrupted. "He was Caliban to your Miranda, my dear young lady.''

"Oh, that's *The Tempest,* is it not?'' she said interestedly.

"Yes, you are quite right. *The Tempest.*'' He smiled at her. "But where are you going, my fair Miranda? Perhaps I could escort you there. Certainly you should not be out here all by yourself.''

"I know I should not,'' Julie sighed. "My abigail is sick . . . else she would have accompanied me.'' She looked up and was alarmed to find him regarding her almost as appreciatively and boldly as her erstwhile tormentor. She continued hastily, "But you need not trouble yourself further, sir. I am going only to the bathing machines.''

"Ah, it is a fine morning for a swim. Do you enjoy battling the surf?''

"I think I might. I have never been in the ocean.''

Julie edged away from him, moving quickly down the boardwalk. "Again I do thank you for your help, sir," she added, wishing that he was not still keeping pace with her.

"You have never been in the ocean?" He raised his eyebrows. "And here I was thinking you a veritable mermaid. Of course, it does not matter whether you can swim or not—if you choose to avail yourself of the bathing machines. You'll not get an opportunity to swim so much as half a stroke. Those old women who operate them are called 'dippers,' as I am sure you must know."

"Dippers?" Julie questioned, not wanting to encourage him but intrigued in spite of herself. "Why are they called so?"

"Because once you are ready to brave the waters, they will drop you and pull you out before you've . . . er . . . flipped your tail."

Julie decided to ignore what she considered to be a slightly off-color sally. "Oh, dear, is that true? I should not like that. I am really a very good swimmer."

"Well, then, my Miranda, you should not be patronizing the dippers. There's another place where the real swimmers go. It is called Scarborough Beach, and there's none will interfere with your enjoyment of the waters. Would you like me to take you there? It is not very far."

There was a look in his eyes and an eagerness to his tone that Julie did not like. She shook her head. "I think I would prefer the bathing machines, at least until I am used to the actions of the sea." She moved away from him, her eyes on the so-called "machines," which were actually no more than tall boxlike structures set on small platforms and harnessed to horses which, even at this distance, appeared to be several years past their prime.

"They are regular nags," her companion commented, almost as if, indeed, he had read her thoughts. "I have never used the bathing machines myself, but judging from the disparaging comments of some of my friends, they are quite uncomfortable. If you would come with me to Scarborough Beach, I am sure you would find the facilities more to your liking. You do not need to plunge into deep water immediately, you know."

Julie said gently, "I have quite set my heart on the bathing machines, sir. I might not enjoy them, I agree, but I think it were best that I discovered that for myself."

He frowned. "You will not welcome the experience, I can assure you," he said coolly. "And—"

"Hey, you there!" someone yelled.

Startled, Julie turned at the sound and tensed as she saw Mr. Travers striding in their direction. "Oh, dear!" she exclaimed.

"Ah, my dear little Miranda, I thought that I had discouraged our Romeo—but methinks the lout is hankering for a second round. I thought that I had floored him permanently in the first."

"I thought so too," Julie sighed.

"He is uncommon persistent. I would have thought that . . ." He stared down at Julie. "Have you led me astray, then, my sweet?"

Julie had been gazing nervously in the direction of the approaching Mr. Travers, but, surprised by his question, she raised her eyes to find his gaze cool and, she thought with some indignation, accusing. "How might I have led you astray, sir?" she demanded.

"I was wondering if, after all, I might not have interfered between a man and his lady fair?"

With a mixture of indignation and disbelief, Julie snapped, "He is nothing to me. I never saw him until I came out on the beach." She glared at Mr. Travers and realized with some dismay that he was even closer.

"Dear, dear, such determination, and with so little encouragement! He is, I think, a hardier spirit than myself. Indeed, I am most reluctant to close with him again. My hand still aches from contact with his bone-box. Still, if you were minded to be a trifle more approachable and come with me to Scarborough Beach, I might yet be your champion."

There was a hard look in his eyes as he proffered the invitation, and Julie, liking him even less than Mr. Travers, said coldly, "I think you must excuse me, sir." Before he had a chance to respond, she had dashed across the beach, and reaching the first of several bathing machines, yanked open the door. Much to her relief, it was empty. A moment later she had hoisted herself inside and slammed the door.

" 'Ere." The door was wrenched open again by a tall rawboned woman in a sea-stained gown, very wet from the waist down. "Wot are ye doin' in 'ere?"

"Please," Julie panted. "I . . . I was on my way here to the machines when a man—"

"Ye need say no more," the woman interrupted. "Ye be a pretty piece'n alone, are ye?"

"My abigail's ill," Julie explained. "I left her at the Old Ship Hotel."

"Um," the woman grunted. "Well, it's not my business. 'Twill be a shillin' for the machine'n another for my services."

"I have the money," Julie assured her hastily. She peered out of the window and stiffened as she saw Mr. Travers striding purposefully across the beach. "Oh, dear!" she exclaimed. "He is still following me. I did not think . . . No matter. Please, please, can we go?"

The woman glanced in the direction Julie had been looking. " 'Im!" she exclaimed in accents of disgust. " 'E be an ugly lout, 'e be. Seen 'im before. Every

pretty girl wot shows 'er face . . . e's after. I'll 'ave
Clarissa 'ere draw ye to the water's edge'n then I'll 'elp
ye to dress." She patted the rear of the horse.

"Do hurry," Julie begged.

"Calm down. 'E'll not be wantin' to tangle wi' Susan
Briggs, I can assure ye." There was a martial light in
Miss Briggs's eyes. "Ye just 'ang on tight to yon
doorknob'n we'll be down to the seashore in minutes."

"I do thank you," Julie breathed.

In the next quarter of an hour, jounced about in a
wooden structure that smelled most unpleasantly of
stale seawater, Julie was still fearful that she might not
have eluded the all-too-persistent Mr. Travers.
Consequently, when the conveyance came to a stop, she
cast a wary glance out of its clouded window. Much to
her relief, she did not see him, and in that same moment
Miss Briggs jerked open the door, thus giving Julie an
exciting look at the frothing surf advancing on and
retreating from the rocky beach.

Giggles and squeals reached her ears, and looking to
her left, she saw another wagon drawn up beside her. A
brawny woman was immersing a young girl in the water
and pulling her up again, keeping a horny hand on the
folds of her flannel bathing costume.

"Ooooooh, Bridey, do not let me go," the girl
shrieked. "I am sure I would drown!"

"Don't ye worry none, miss," the woman yelled.
"Old Bridey wouldn't let that 'appen."

Julie bit down a giggle. There was little chance that
the occupant of the next machine could drown in what
appeared to be no more than a foot of water.

" 'Ere," her own handmaiden rasped. "I'll 'elp ye
dress. Be it in this 'ere bag?" Without waiting for
Julie's reply, she plunged her hand into the bag and
drew out the blue-and-white flannel garment that the
mantau-maker had insisted was the very latest in modish

swimming attire. Fastened by drawstrings at the neck, it was as full and commodious as the bedgown it so closely resembled. With it was a gathered cap to protect the hair.

Once garbed in this costume, Julie felt sadly encumbered as, at Miss Briggs's command, she stepped down from the cart onto the beach. A vision of the sequestered lake where she had learned to swim was in her mind. There, she had worn nothing at all, and it had been very pleasant feeling the chill waters coursing over her bare skin. These memories were rudely banished by a thrust from her companion.

"In ye go!" Miss Briggs shrilled.

Julie, falling to her knees, was doused by an incoming wave. Water filled her eyes, her nose, and her mouth, leaving her coughing, spluttering, and indignant as Miss Briggs, a hand on the collar of her soaking gown, yanked her up.

" 'Ow do ye like it?" she demanded.

"You should have warned me," Julie began, only to be thrust into the water a second time, and before she could do so much as move her arms in a swimming motion, she was summarily pulled out.

"Please," she managed to splutter. "I can swim, you know. You can let me go now."

"Not on yer life, miss. 'Twould be as much as me position's worth. I've 'ad them wot said as 'ow they could swim'n next thing I know, I'm pumpin' most the sea from 'em."

Meeting the dipper's kindling eye, Julie regretfully abandoned her arguments. However, when finally the experience was at an end, she resolved never to repeat it. Never, she reasoned ruefully, had she been so aware of her diminutive size! She had been no match for Miss Briggs's superior strength, and to be pushed in and hastily pulled out of those enticing green waters had been incredibly frustrating and unpleasant, as well. Indeed, it was quite as unpleasant as the man who rescued her from Mr. Travers had implied. As she parted from the dipper, something else he had mentioned came to mind.

"Where is Scarborough Beach?" she inquired.

Miss Briggs stiffened and gave her a lowering and, at the same time, probing look. "Why'd you want to be knowin' that?"

"I have heard that they do not have bathing machines there," Julie said bravely. There was also a touch of defiance to her tone as she continued, "I would like to go someplace where I would be able to swim!"

"Hah!" Miss Briggs exclaimed. "I might be mistook, but it seems to me that a young lady o' yer breedin' wouldn't like swimmin' stark naked'n wi' all the gentlemen turnin' their spyglasses on you."

Julie reddened. "No, I cannot say that I would."

"Oo was it told you about it?" Miss Briggs demanded fiercely. "I'd lay you a monkey 'twas the man wot scared you."

Julie nodded, deciding that it would not be too far from the truth to say, "Yes, that is true."

Miss Briggs shook her head. "It's best you 'ightail it back to yer lodgin'-'ouse. Anyone can see you ain't up to snuff'n furthermore there's a big blow a-comin' up. Look at the clouds swirlin' about—you'll be caught in a storm if you don't 'urry."

"I will hurry," Julie assured her gratefully. "Thank you very much, Miss Briggs."

She had every intention by abiding by Miss Briggs's well-meant and undoubtedly wise counsel, but as Julie started up the sloping beach in the direction of the boardwalk, she saw a tall man standing near the steps. His outlines appeared all too familiar, and though, at this distance, she could not discern his features, she had a very queasy feeling that he might respond to the name of Travers.

At present, he was standing quite motionless, but it seemed to her that he was staring directly at her. Still, she could not be sure. She took another tentative step and came to a startled stop as a fierce gust of wind took her breath away. Evidently Miss Briggs's "big blow" was on the way! She must get to the boardwalk, but she had taken no more than another step when, to her consternation, the man came swiftly down to the beach. Julie froze. It was Mr. Travers, and she could discern a black frown on his face. With a gasp of fright she turned swiftly, running blindly away from him, moving as fast as she might, given the shifting rocks beneath her feet.

"You . . . you little wretch! It is you, blast and damn you," he yelled.

As his words reached her, she knew that even as she had been uncertain of his identity, he had been similarly confused. She increased her speed, and despite the wind in her face, seemed to be making headway. She was relieved to find herself headed toward the shore. She must reach it as soon as possible. The beach was flatter there and consequently better for running. In another few moments she had gained the water's edge. Standing there for a moment, she endeavored to catch her breath and, at the same time, gather enough strength to run again. It was very hard to run, especially after her semi-combat with the dipper. Still, she dared not stop. Her destination, the Old Ship Hotel, was not very far, but it would mean changing direction and plodding uphill again.

"Love," came a spent voice behind her. "At last . . ."

Glancing over her shoulder, Julie felt her heart pounding in her throat. He was no more than a few feet distant, and though he had addressed her affectionately, she read fury in his eyes. With a little squeal of fright she started running again.

"My dear," he called. "Stop. The game's at an end. It's time we went back to our hotel."

She turned cold. He was pretending they were playing a game, that they were friends—more than friends. She could not dwell on that. She must keep running, and in that moment she slipped and fell. Before she could scramble to her feet, a small spent wave rolled up, momentarily engulfing her feet and her legs and thoroughly wetting the bottom half of her gown and cloak.

"My dear," he called. "Did you hurt yourself? Here . . . let me help you."

Julie cast another glance behind her and saw that he was no more than a hundred feet away. Unmindful of the water in her shoes and her soaking skirt and cloak, she began to run again. A glance to her right showed her that there were people on the beach—but were she to appeal to them would any of them spring to her defense as had the man earlier? And if they did, might they not pursue her also? She increased her speed, and looking over her shoulder again, trembled. He was still striding purposefully in her direction and the distance between them was even narrower. Once more she endeavored to increase her speed, and suddenly came upon two boys pushing a rowboat toward the water. Reaching them, Julie gasped, "The boat . . . I must come with you."

They stared at her in what, surprisingly enough, appeared to be fright. "Be . . . be it yours?" one of them asked.

She divined their fears. They must have found the boat, which undoubtedly was the property of someone else. A hasty glance downward assured her that it was equipped with oars. "Yes, of course it is mine!" she snapped. Suiting her actions to her assertion, she pushed it toward the water and, in a matter of moments, had climbed into it and was letting the waves bear her out to sea.

"You . . . you . . . you . . ." came an angry cry behind her. "Come back."

Was it her pursuer or was it the rightful owner of the boat? Unlike Lot's wife, Julie did not glance back. Lifting first one and then the other oar from its lock, she shoved them into the water and began to row, breasting the breakers with the one purpose of going beyond them and remaining there until her enemy tired of his pursuit.

Fortunately, she was not unacquainted with rowboats. There had been one on the lake at home. Her father had taught her how to handle it. Her only fear was that she might be borne back by a swelling wave—borne back to the man who, with such fell intent, awaited her on what had suddenly become a most unfriendly shore.

4

Julie guided her boat beyond the breakers. She encountered little opposition, for, unlike the lake, where on occasion her arms had ached from the exertion of rowing, she seemed to be skimming over the waters with remarkable ease. She did not even need to use her oars. A strong current bore her forward. She might even find herself nearing the yachts, she thought, and was vaguely aware of shouts from the shore. She did not look back. She could imagine Mr. Travers' anger. She could also envision his lowering expression. Indeed, he did not look unlike an angry bull. He had much the same tactic—to charge and knock down. If she had remained and he had caught up with her, which, inevitably, he must have done, for she had been tired, the backs of her legs were still aching from her dash across the beach . . . but she must not think of that. She must needs turn her mind to finding a place where she might bring her boat ashore. That would present difficulties, she feared, because she might have trouble finding her way back to the hotel, and poor Lucy would be frantic!

She cast a look over her shoulder and to her surprise found the shore even further away than she had anticipated. In that same moment, the boat seemed to drop way down, and then it rose up to a height that startled her. Cresting a wave, the boat went down again, and though she plied her oars expertly, they were proving to be of little use. The wind was blowing harder and the waves were even higher. The water must be very deep here, she thought nervously, and in the same moment she saw a yacht. It was quite a distance away, but still, it was close enough so that she could read the name on the prow. *Diana.*

Diana, goddess of the hunt and the moon, Julie recalled. It was not, she decided, a very suitable name for a ship. A ship ought to be called after Neptune or some goddess of the sea—Aphrodite was born in the sea . . . a great shell. There was a painting her father had described. He had seen it in Italy on his honeymoon. Wonderful to go to Italy . . . she had always wanted to see different parts of the world. Diana. It might be a woman's name, a woman beloved of the yacht's owner —his wife, sailing with him around the island called Britain . . . Her thoughts fled. Another wave was rising before her. It seemed as high as a church steeple and she must either breast it or be engulfed!

She thrust her oars into those dark green depths and felt the force of the increasing wind at her back. She must, must, *must* try to get back to shore, but on looking over her shoulder again, she could no longer see the shore! She could see only veritable cliffs of water! She had never rowed such a distance . . . but she had not really rowed at all, she realized. There had been no need to thrust her oars into that roiling sea. The action of the waters had sufficed, and now they seemed to wrest her oars from her hands. Wet and hard against her palms one moment, they were gone the next, inexorably swept away by the same wave that was tossing the boat about like a toy ship on the Serpentine! In another second it had tilted, sending Julie into the water, down into the water, down, down, down beneath the waves!

Coughing and spluttering, her eyes, her ears, her nose, and her mouth streaming water, she battled her way to the surface and saw the boat bobbing out of reach. Her skirt was heavy about her legs, her cloak heavier, binding them, but she managed to keep afloat, staring about her with water-blurred eyes. The boat was floating further away, but with a thrust of her feet she desperately drove herself forward and was able to clutch its tilting side, and despite the pull of the waters, to hang on. Her throat was suddenly hoarse from screams she hardly remembered having uttered. She screamed again, and then again, again, again, futilely, she knew, for the sounds were carried away by the howling winds—but still she felt the hardness of the boat beneath her hands and must not let go, else she would once more be dragged down into those green depths, never, never to rise again!

Of a sudden, Julie was vaguely aware of another sound, a hoarse voice, but there could be no voices here. Something clutched her. She struggled and screamed against that determined hold and knew it must be Mr. Travers who had found his way across the waters and caught her, snared her in his nets. He would take her, she knew not where—she knew only that she was in terrible danger and must fight against his determined hands, continue to fight, but then she felt a hard blow to her chin and knew nothing more.

Voices, men's voices, rising and falling, were in her ears, and beneath her was a peculiar motion—one she could not define. She felt . . . But it was difficult to ascertain her exact feelings. A chaotic sense of displacement had invaded her mind. Fragmented images skittered behind her eyes—a memory of a beach and herself running, running, was superimposed upon dark waters, green and tall. Water was never tall. It lay flat on the lake. Not the lake, the sea . . . a sea of wind-whipped waves . . . and she tossed upon them like a piece of driftwood, and Mr. Travers . . . Who was Mr. Travers? He had captured her, she remembered with a rising fear, and now she lay in darkness. She groaned aloud as she envisioned his face, his eyes, his dark eyes boring into her.

"I think she be comin' round, my lord."

The voice, low and rumbling, entered Julie's ears. It was vaguely familiar. Her confusion increased.

"What could she have been doing, out in a rowboat in the midst of that windstorm?"

The second voice, edged by a mixture of curiosity and . . . Could she call it impatience or annoyance? She was not sure, she was sure only that it was a beautifully modulated voice, deep and somehow reassuring. It could not belong to Mr. Travers was her next thought, and concurrent with that she was experiencing a sense of self, a sense of being alive and knowing that she had anticipated death. With a determined effort she gathered her thoughts and knew that the darkness about her was of her own making—because her eyes were shut. With an effort, she opened them to a dimness, to a round window directly ahead of her or, rather, her aroused mind supplied, a porthole! She was on a ship! Into her mind sped an image of that white yacht and the name *Diana*.

"Di . . . Di . . ." she mumbled, finding that her tongue seemed heavy and weighted, preventing her from expressing herself clearly.

"Ah," said the deep voice. "You are right. She has regained consciousness."

"Yes," Julie affirmed, glad that this second word came more easily than the first, with its utterance, her thoughts finally coalesced. "Rescued . . ." she muttered. "Not drowned."

"No, my poor child," the beautiful voice assured her. "By a great stroke of fortune, you are alive, and when

you are better . . . But never mind that now. 'Tis best
you do not try to think. My steward has brought some
broth . . . you must drink it, and afterward, sleep.
You'll be the better for a long sleep.''

"Yes,'' Julie agreed out of her increasing confusion.
She did not want to sleep, not yet. She had questions
that must needs be answered—but she did feel so weary,
weary and drained of strength. Indeed, when a spoonful
of a very tasty broth was pressed between her lips, she
could barely swallow it and, indeed, was thankful when
the feeding ceased and she could return to the darkness
from which she had so briefly emerged. Yet even as it
descended, she was aware of her continued existence
and of the deep, beautiful voice that had first assured
her of it.

Julie's second awakening brought her a vivid memory
of the events leading up to her current plight. She had
opened her eyes to a cabin bathed in the rosy, wavering
light of a rising sun and to an initial feeling of over-
whelming relief. She was alive . . . alive, when she had
been positive that death awaited her in the waters of that
windswept sea. However, as she moved restlessly, she
was aware of something hampering her movements. She
looked beneath the covers and found she was wearing a
sort of shirt that reached no further than her knees. It
was large for her; the sleeves engulfed her arms and
hung over her hands. It must be a shirt lent to her by the
man with the voice. And where were her own clothes?
They must be drying out. Yet, who had undressed her?
She could not dwell on that—there were matters more
important that must engage her mind. Where could she
be?

She had a ready answer for that. She was on a ship
going she knew not whither, and, furthermore, a night
and part of a day had passed. Lucy would be frantic!

She must think . . . But what could the poor girl think? She had not been aware of Julie's departure, and were she to make inquiries, who would provide answers to her panic-stricken queries?

Lucy knew she wanted to go swimming. She might approach the dippers, might speak to Miss Briggs— but even if the woman recognized the description and agreed that she had waited on her, she would not be able to supply any additional information.

There were also the boys with the rowboat. However, it was extremely unlikely that either of them would come forward, and, of course, there was Mr. Travers, who had seen her rowing out to sea. There was a chance that he would report her drowning, but there was an even greater chance that he would not, and Lucy, poor Lucy, would be convinced that she had vanished from the face of the earth. She would acquaint Julie's family with that intelligence and her brother Raymond would hasten to lay claim to her inheritance!

"No," she whispered. He could not. He would have to wait until her death was established. Meanwhile, she would acquaint the man with the voice, the captain, possibly, with her plight and he could drop her at some adjacent port and surely he could spare the money that would bring her safely back to Brighton. She released a caught breath and, oddly, felt sleep coming upon her, but she must not sleep. She must rise immediately and seek the owner of the yacht and . . . She closed her eyes and lost her battle with Morpheus.

"Two days!" Julie, standing in a large, beautifully appointed cabin, looked incredulously at the man whom, Mr. Champley, his first mate, had recently and reverently introduced as Richard Neville, Earl of Aylsford, the owner and captain of the yacht *Diana*.

In the beautifully modulated voice that had made

such an impression on her even when half-drowned, his
lordship assured Julie that she had, indeed, been
sleeping for the better part of two days, waking only to
partake of the tea and soup his steward had forced her
to drink.

"But where are we?" she asked, her mind supplying a
host of images, these still dominated by Lucy's concern
and the confusion of her family.

"We are within little more than a day of our destination," Lord Aylsford said soothingly. "I speak of our
specific destination, of course. I am bound for
Cornwall."

"Cornwall!" Julie exclaimed, her benumbed brain
proving quite unable to ascertain the distance between
Brighton and Cornwall. "But there must be a port . . ."
she began, and paused, looking down, aware of her sea-
faded garments, mute evidence of her ordeal. If she had
needed any reminding, they told her of her position
aboard this yacht. She was at a great disadvantage! She
had actually been about to ask him to go out of his way
and leave her at some port where she might begin her
journey back to Brighton—but for that, she would need
funds, funds to pay the fare and to buy new clothes,
and, again, she would have to borrow those funds from
him!

"I have the impression that you are . . . rather
confused, Miss . . . Carlington, is it?"

"It is Carleton, sir. Julie—Julia Carleton."

"Miss Carleton, then. And I must needs admit to
confusion myself. What were you doing so far from
shore—in a rowboat and with a storm coming up?"

Julie read more than mere confusion in that candid
gaze. She had an uncomfortable suspicion that he
thought her either lacking in sense or, worse, slightly
mad. She said defensively, "I had not meant to be . . .
but he, Mr. Travers . . . he was so angry and I was

afraid . . . There was no one to whom I could turn, and he was gaining on me.''

"He was gaining on you?"

She grimaced. "I see that I am not making any sense at all, my lord. I will begin at the beginning, if I may.''

"Please do, Miss Carleton.''

Haltingly she explained the situation. "I expect I ought to have brought my abigail,'' she finished lamely, "but I never expected that those gentlemen would act so oddly.''

He gave her a penetrating stare. "You are not used to such odd behavior, Miss Carleton?''

"No, sir. I cannot think what occasioned it,'' she said candidly.

"You have never had a similar experience?''

"No, sir . . . er, my lord,'' she said in some surprise, for his tone as well as his glance had been skeptical. Indeed, she had the uncomfortable feeling that he did not believe her.

"Where have you been living, Miss Carleton?'' he inquired.

"At home, my lord. Outside of Chilham.''

"Ah, Kent.'' He nodded. "And how long have you been residing there, may I ask?''

Since it was hardly necessary to mention her brief unhappy two months in London, Julie said, "All my life, sir.''

"Ummmmm, I expect that is an explanation, though, for myself, I still find it strange. But no matter, I do wish I could take you back to Brighton. Unfortunately, time being of the essence as far as I am concerned, I cannot leave you at a port between here and Cornwall. We have been much delayed by weather and I am on the way to meet my promised bride.

"Still, I wish to assure you that you need not be concerned for your reputation. Once we have arrived at

Truro, which is on the way to the home of my future father-in-law, Sir Nigel Penrose, I will see that you board the stage and we will concoct some tale to assuage the fears of your family and save your reputation. No one need know that you were aboard my yacht." A flush mounted his cheeks. "I fear that I am known as a rake in certain parts of this country, namely London. However, all that is at an end. I am to be married in three weeks' time, and needless to say, I am turning over a new leaf." A slight smile curled his lips and gleamed briefly from his eyes.

The information he had given her was hardly welcome, especially when she thought of poor Lucy, stranded in Brighton and not knowing where to turn. It was also possible that she had gone back to the Manor to break the news to the family. Would they imagine her dead? She could not dwell on that now. Lord Aylsford was looking at her anxiously and she did not want to add to his worries by citing her own. Consequently she must needs put a good face on the matter and, at the same time, reassure him that he need not fear any challenges from the male members of her family, a possibility that might have crossed his mind.

"I do thank you, my lord," she said. She found she could smile at him quite easily, as she continued, "I beg you will not worry about any possible repercussions from my family. They will not be concerned about my reputation because, quite frankly, I have none."

He regarded her with no little surprise. "I am not quite sure that I catch your meaning, Miss Carleton," he said after a slight pause.

"I am divorced, my lord, divorced and disgraced. There was quite a furor about it some years back. My husband is, or rather was, Sir Edwin Fitzroy."

He frowned and then gave a brief nod which Julie interpreted as a stirred memory of that scandalous divorce. However, he said merely, "I imagine that I must have been out of London at the time, Lady Fitzroy."

Julie winced. "Please," she said hastily, "I have not used that name in years. I am plain Julie Carleton."

There was a flicker of amusement in his dark eyes. "I could never call you 'plain,' Miss Carleton."

She blushed. "I was only trying to explain . . ."

"I understand what you are trying to explain and also to convey, Miss Carleton, and I thank you for relieving my mind. I see I will not have to face an enraged father or brother . . . though were I related to you . . ." He reddened. "But be that as it may, Miss Carleton, no word of this, er . . . adventure will ever escape my lips or those of my crew, and the shreds of your reputation will, at least, remain intact."

"You are indeed kind, my lord," she said softly. "I hope I have not delayed your wedding journey."

"It cannot yet be called a 'wedding journey,' Miss Carleton. It is a voyage to the place of my wedding." His eyes were briefly somber. "I will be marrying a young lady whom I have not seen since I was thirteen and she seven."

"Oh, my goodness!" Julie exclaimed. "It must be an arranged marriage too." She had spoken impulsively and with a sympathy that she immediately regretted. "I mean—"

"I imagine," he interrupted, "that you meant exactly what you said, and it is true. This marriage was arranged between our parents many years ago."

"Mine was also arranged, my brothers' and sisters' marriages as well," she said, adding hastily, "theirs— all of them—turned out most satisfactorily."

His smile was slightly twisted. "Are you endeavoring to give me some belated reassurances, Miss Carleton? That is kind, especially in light of your own experience."

There was no misreading the bitterness in his tone.

Evidently the marriage was not entirely to his liking. Family pressures had probably been brought to bear, and Julie found herself feeling very sorry for him. However, before she could utter the words of consolation forming on her tongue, there was a knock at the door, and at the earl's question, Mr. Champley hurried in to say that another storm was blowing up.

Seeing concern leap into the earl's eyes, Julie hastily excused herself and went back to her cabin. There was a brisk wind blowing and the crew was busy with the sails, but despite her earlier peril, Julie, reaching her cabin, found herself dwelling on her brief conversation with Lord Aylsford, or, more specifically, she was envisioning the play of emotion on his handsome features. He was extremely handsome, almost beautiful. She had always admired dark eyes and coal-black hair. Or had she?

To be absolutely truthful, she had not realized how very felicitous such coloring could be until she had set eyes on the earl. Furthermore, though he was tall—ten or eleven inches over five feet—he was not excessively tall, something she appreciated since she herself was so small. She had always felt at a great disadvantage with Edwin, who had been a gigantic six-feet-two and hefty. He had always given her the impression of looking down on her, even before those terrible moments after Sir James Massinger had brought her home on that fatal morning. She shuddered, recalling the expression on Edwin's face as he towered over her, recalling, too, his contemptuous words, each one seemingly bitten off and spat at her.

Lord Aylsford, no matter how angry he was, could never have looked at a woman that way, and nor could he have spoken to her as if she were some erring servant girl—she was sure of that! Indeed, she wished . . . Julie stiffened in shock at the wish she had stolen into her mind. It was of a nature she had not entertained in years, not since she was fifteen or sixteen.

Edwin Fitzroy had been no more than a name on her mother's lips in those days, and she had been caught up in the tales of Sir Lancelot and Sir Gawain. Once she had even lain flat in a rowboat on the lake pretending that she was the hapless Elaine floating down to Camelot. She winced. A keeper had sighted her and, in a fright, had rowed out and pulled the boat to shore. Despite her frantic pleas, he had reported the incident to her governess, who had summarily conveyed the tale to her mother.

Julie preferred not to dwell on the contempt in Lady Carleton's voice as she had banished her to her room for the rest of the week and confiscated the book. Still, it was not her mother who had put an end to her taste for romance. That dream had died on her wedding day and had been buried forever that same night. She had never experienced so much as a twinge of those forgotten emotions until . . . But she must not forget that in three weeks Lord Aylsford would be married to a young lady he barely knew and would live unhappily ever after—or perhaps not, if she were beautiful and gentle and kind. Tears sprang to her eyes, and then a loud crash of thunder, coupled with a lurch of the ship sending her hurtfully to her knees, dispersed Julie's thoughts, thoughts which, she realized ruefully, she ought never to have entertained.

The storm, springing up out of nowhere, was frightening in its intensity but brief in duration, calming down late in the afternoon—though at its height, the earl, clad in oilskins, had knocked at Julie's cabin door to assure her that its sound was worse than its impact. Still, upon shakily emerging from her cabin, Julie found that there were a broken mast and other sundry damages, these being explained to her by a boatswain, who, despite what she feared to be a most serious situation, spoke very jovially.

Additional insight into the matter was provided by another young seaman, who volunteered to take Julie to the spot where a spar had fallen. To her surprise, he sounded almost cheerful as he also volunteered the information that they had been blown off course and must needs put into some adjacent port for repairs. He was explaining the nature of those repairs in considerable technical detail, aided by a comrade, who was helpfully translating the information into terms she might more readily understand—when of a sudden, the earl appeared, saying coldly, "That will be enough, Metford, and you, Jones, have you no work awaiting you?"

Looking abashed, the two men hurried away as the earl, turning to Julie, said with equal coldness, "If you have questions concerning the damage to the vessel, Miss Carleton, it were better that they were addressed to me."

"I did not question them, my lord, they volunteered the information," Julie responded edgily, not liking the reproach she heard in his tone.

"I am sure they did." He smiled then. "And I must beg your pardon, I see."

"You have it, my lord," she responded, realizing in that moment and with considerable relief that the emotions he had originally aroused in her breast seemed to have been blown out to sea with the storm—or was it the peremptory way he had addressed her just now that had served to vanquish those early and unwelcome sensations? Something in his manner had reminded her strongly of the accusatory way her mother had been wont to speak to her, and also her husband.

" . . . tomorrow morning," he concluded.

Julie, realizing belatedly that the earl had been

addressing her, was embarrassed. She had no notion of what he had been saying. Consequently, hoping for further enlightenment, she merely nodded.

"Very good," he said. "You will be ready at nine tomorrow morning, then?"

"Of course," she assented. "And will you take me to the stagecoach then?"

He looked surprised. "No, not tomorrow." He gave her a narrow look. "Were you attending to what I was just telling you, Miss Carleton?"

Julie, feeling her face burn, said, "I . . . fear my wits were wandering, my lord. The . . . the storm, you know."

"I understand." He visited another narrow look on her face. "I am sure it must have been frightening, especially coming upon your very recent escape from death."

"Yes, very," she agreed on a note of relief. "And what were you saying?"

"We will need to go ashore tomorrow. I must find someone who can help my crew make the repairs to the vessel. And if you ask me why I do not delegate this errand to one of my men, I will tell you that I prefer to handle these matters myself."

"I see," she said. "And why do you wish me to accompany you, my lord?"

"Can you not guess?" he demanded.

"No," she said on a note of surprise.

He surveyed her in silence for a moment before saying, "Well, Miss Carleton, since I am beginning to believe that you are without guile, I must tell you that judging from the reactions of my crew, I prefer not to leave you on board in my absence. I doubt if you would sustain any harm from my men, but when a woman is young and beautiful, she is a source of controversy, if not temptation. Does that answer your question?"

Julie, her face uncomfortably warm, stuttered, "I . . . I am not very young, s-sir . . . er, my lord, and as for being beautiful . . ."

"If you attempt to deny either, you will get a strong argument from me, Miss Carleton." He frowned. "And I might tell you that I really dislike false modesty."

It was Julie's turn to frown. She said coldly, "I am not falsely modest, my lord. I am three months past my twenty-fifth birthday."

"And I"—he regarded her quizzically—"have reached my twenty-ninth year. I am not, however, prepared to call myself aged. But be that as it may, Miss Carleton, I must beg that you excuse me. It is necessary to confer with my first mate, and may I hope that you will accompany me ashore tomorrow?"

The change from command to request was not lost on Julie, and since she also appreciated the reasons behind that invitation and was loath to experience even a semblance of the situation that had sent her into that rowboat, she said, "I will, my lord."

5

Meeting his lordship at precisely nine in the morning, Julie found him neatly garbed in buckskin breeches, a dark blue coat, and a plain white waistcoat. His boots were polished to a high shine and his cravat, she noted with approval, was plainly tied. Edwin, she recalled, had always insisted on intricate folds and a great deal of starch. The result had looked very uncomfortable given his short neck—but why was she comparing the two men? As well compare Caliban to Prospero!

"I will be rowing us ashore, Miss Carleton," he said, pointing to a small boat much akin to the one in which she had sustained her near-fatal accident. "I could not spare any of my men. We do not have a large crew and there are many repairs to be made." He added dubiously, "I hope we will be able to find assistance here. It is not much of a village."

Looking out across the water, Julie saw a rocky beach stretching up to a few cottages, all of which bore the mark of the raging elements. Though she was inclined to agree with him, she said, "There must be some able-bodied men about."

"We can hope—else my future father-in-law will think me lost at sea."

"We *have* reached Cornwall," she reminded him.

"So we have, Miss Carleton, and can take pleasure in

that, at least. And now," he continued, "we have a choice . . ." His eyes were on a stretch of sand, and beside it, some rough wooden steps. "Do you trust nature or man?"

"Nature," Julie said promptly.

He laughed. "You were quick in taking my meaning, and I am in agreement—rather sand than splinters."

As they trudged up the incline, Julie looked about her and was conscious that she was being observed, not only by the people in the street. Her quick eye caught fingers holding curtains aside in the houses they were beginning to pass as they gained the summit of the incline. "I do not think they like us," Julie commented in a low voice.

"I am of the opinion that they do not like strangers, Miss Carleton. How many people do you know who can say that they have been to Cornwall?"

"None, that I know," Julie responded. "But my acquaintance has been rather curtailed in the last few years."

He regarded her in silence for a moment and then said half teasingly, "Ah, yes, 'Reputation, reputation, reputation!' I quote Cassio—and I am rather sure that neither of you deserved that blight."

"Oh, I expect I deserved it," Julie said frankly. "Though I cannot be absolutely sure—since I have no memory of that evening at all."

He came to a stop. "None?" he questioned, a slight frown between his eyes.

"No, you see, I had taken far too much to drink."

"Had you taken it or had it been pressed upon you?"

"It was pressed," she said. "You see, I was looking down at the floor . . . everyone was dancing, and the different costumes were so bright and gay. There were so many different peoples represented—Arabs and Chinese and Gypsies . . . there were some beautiful medieval costumes too, and one man was clad in a full suit of armor! I remember that my glass never seemed to be empty . . . it surprised me at the time, for I thought that I had taken quite a bit . . . but it was always full, and obviously it was far too much, because I can recall nothing of the evening—the rest of the evening, I mean. All I know is that I must have gone home with Sir James Massinger, because on the following morning I . . . I awoke in his . . . room." She had been about to say "bed," but to her surprise, her tongue, usually the willing servant of her quick mind, stumbled over the word "bed" and stopped with "room."

"I see," he said.

"I do not expect that you do," Julie said matter-of-factly. "I was extremely surprised myself, but no one believed me. They thought . . . " She hesitated and then continued, "Well, the judge granted the divorce and gave his sincere sympathies to Edwin, whom he described as 'unfortunate.' "

"I see," he repeated.

Julie swallowed a small sigh. "I expect it is difficult to believe me." She spoke thoughtfully. "No one in the family did, only my father later decided to forgive me."

"I am glad to hear it. The others did not?"

"Oh, no," Julie said. "You see, they could not enjoy the Manor with me present. They did not want their children to meet me and . . . " She paused. "I begin to think that I am talking too much."

"On the contrary, Miss Carleton, you have both my ears and my full attention," he said gravely. "But I expect that we must continue into the village, time being of the essence."

"Yes, your bride will certainly be impatient," Julie observed, and felt a queer little thump in the region of her throat, or was it a pulsing or a sort of closed sob? She was not sure, but it did not matter or, rather, it did,

and she did know what had occasioned it and must not
dwell on the subject. She hastened her steps—which
meant dropping his arm—and reached the top of the hill
before he did.

The earl joined her quickly. "I beg you will not dart
away from me, Miss Carleton," he said edgily. "You
have already learned how difficult it can be when you
are not accompanied."

She flushed. "But you were directly behind me," she
pointed out.

He did not answer immediately. He was looking
about him. There were very few people on the streets
and those who were present all seemed to be hurrying in
the other direction, as if, indeed, they were intent upon
avoiding the newcomers.

"I hope," the earl said in a low voice, "that we will
not be long in securing assistance. I have not been in
Cornwall for many years, but I seem to remember that
they are not particularly friendly to strangers, and these,
I must admit, seem even less friendly than most."

"They do," Julie agreed. "They seem almost frightened."

"Since neither of us is an ogre, I will hope that you
are exaggerating." He looked about him. "Now, where
do you think we can find help? I imagine it is best to try
one of the larger houses." Taking her arm, he started up
a street which, in common with the others, grew steeper
the further they walked.

Julie was feeling rather breathless by the time her
companion stopped in front of a two-story house with a
thatched roof and with a neat garden around it. A
graveled walk led up to an oaken door.

"This looks quite promising," he remarked.
"Come." Taking Julie's arm, he hurried her up to the
door. It was centered by a knocker in the shape of a
huge fish. Lord Aylsford lifted it, and rather than

letting it fall, thrust it against its plate so that the sound, louder than usual, lingered in Julie's ears.

It was a moment before the door opened and a woman, better dressed than some of those Julie had seen on the street, faced them, her eyes narrowed and her lips turned down. The earl started to speak, only to have the door slammed in his face. With an involuntary little cry, Julie leapt back, and might have lost her footing on the steps had not he caught her arm. "Are you all right?" he said concernedly.

"Quite," she assured him. "I was only surprised."

"As was I. I hope we may not call this a Cornish welcome?"

"As you said earlier, perhaps they are not friendly to strangers."

"I had a feeling," he mused, "that she might have been afraid of us. This is a small place. Perhaps they are not often visited by outsiders. But let us hope that we receive better treatment from one of her neighbors."

They had gone a few more steps when the earl, looking down a side road said, "There is an even larger house . . . at least by the standards of this village. Come, Miss Carleton."

Julie was cheered by a pretty garden and by the fact that this house was whitewashed and its shutters painted a vivid blue to match its roof. The knocker proved to be a brass schooner in full sail. As he lifted it, the earl muttered, "This looks well for our quest."

His summons was answered by a tall, thin man who, Julie thought nervously, regarded them both quite as suspiciously as that ill-mannered woman in the other house. However, he made no move to slam the door in their faces. He listened quietly to Lord Aylsford's explanation of his plight.

"And you're anchored in the harbor, eh?"

"A short distance out of the harbor, sir," the earl

responded. "If you might suggest some men . . ."

The man hesitated, staring at them out of dark, mistrustful eyes set in a thin dark face. His skin, Julie noted, was very dark, reminding her that there was a strong trace of Spanish in many Cornishmen. She also noted that he was still looking at them suspiciously.

He said, "Well, there'll be a number o' young men who might help you, sir. I'll have my nephew hunt them out, and meanwhile, perhaps you and your lady'd stop for a dish of tea?"

The earl looked surprised. "It's kind of you . . . but if you could tell me where I might find them, sir . . ."

"You'd have a sight too much walkin' to do. My nephew's fleet as a hare. It won't take him any time at all." He was smiling now, an expression, Julie noted, that did not reach his eyes. Judging from their earlier experience with a villager, she guessed that distrust might be habitual to the Cornish folk. The earl was evidently of that same opinion, for he thanked the man and said to Julie, "I see no reason why we should not wait here." He glanced at their would-be host. "I hope it will not be too long, sir. We are, of course, grateful for your hospitality, but our ship took a bad beating in the storm and we have still quite a way to sail."

"It will not be overlong, sir," the man replied, a thread of eagerness in his tone. "I beg you will come in."

They entered a small, dimly lighted hall. Directly in front of them was a stairway, the steps highly polished. The floor was similarly polished and a smell of beeswax hung in the air. Their host, who had not yet introduced himself, Julie realized, pulled open a door to their left. There was an eagerness and an urgency to the tone in which he said, "You may wait in here. My wife will bring you the tea. Meanwhile, I'll alert Jem to your needs."

The chamber they entered was also small and furnished with only four cane-bottomed chairs and a round table. However, there was a bowl of orange flowers on the table which lent a touch of needed color to a chamber that was almost oppressively brown—the paneling on walls and floor and door and even the curtains at a pair of mullioned windows were of that hue. Indicating the chairs, their host said, "Will you not sit down? My wife will be with you presently."

"I thank you," the earl responded. "This will prove a pleasant respite after our long climb from the sea."

"From the sea, yes," their host responded in what to Julie's ears was a peculiar tone of voice, almost as if he were laughing. However, before she had time to ponder further on an attitude she was finding exceedingly and increasingly perplexing, the man stepped hastily to the door, saying, "My wife will be with you presently." He hurried out, closing the door with a slam that rattled the glass in the windows, and in another second there was the sound of a key turning in the lock.

"Good God!" The earl strode to the door and pulled at the knob, futilely. He turned back to Julie. "We are locked in!"

She regarded him in consternation, fighting against a rising panic. "Do you suppose . . . ?" she began, and broke off confusedly as she found herself quite unable to fathom the actions of their so-called host.

"I do not know what to suppose!" The earl strode back to the door and pounded on it, saying loudly, "What is the meaning of this, sir? I pray that you will explain this . . . this imprisonment!"

There was only silence. He looked back at Julie, anger and confusion mirrored in his gaze. "I'll be damned if I . . ." He reddened. "I beg your pardon, Miss Carleton." Moving to the windows, he tried to open first one and then the other, but they proved fast

shut. "Blast the rogue, does he mean to suffocate us?"
he said furiously.

"I think not," Julie observed equably. "There is the
fireplace, and I expect air comes through the chimney."

He looked at her in surprise. "I must say that you are
mighty calm about this." Before she had a chance to
reply, he had taken a chair and slammed it against the
door, but it remained unyielding. However, in that same
moment a voice from the hall reached them faintly.
" 'Twill do you no good to try to escape. I have you
fast, the two of you. And you'll stay put till the militia
comes."

"I tell you . . ." the earl shouted.

"And I tell you," their captor yelled back, "ye'll
have cause to rue the day you ever set foot here. News
travels quicker'n you might think, my fine sir."

With another futile pull at the doorknob, the earl
turned away with a rueful look for Julie. "It's a matter
of mistaken identity, it seems. We've but to wait until
they come. I beg you will not be afraid, Miss Carleton."

"I am not afraid, my lord," Julie said. "Obviously
we have not fallen into the hands of some robber baron.
It is an honest error, I am sure."

A warm smile displaced the grimness of his mouth.
"That is a most sensible conclusion, Miss Carleton—
and I must thank you for not treating me to an attack of
the vapors."

"Come, my lord," she chided. "Have I proved
myself so poor-spirited a female?"

He did not respond immediately. Instead, he con-
templated her in silence for a moment before saying
slowly and thoughtfully, "No, Miss Carleton, you have
not. Indeed, I find you a female of amazing fortitude."

His compliment was very pleasant to one who had
had very little praise from anyone save her late father.
She said over an unexpected lump in her throat, "I . . . I
thank you, my lord."

A silence fell between them, and despite her brave words, Julie could not quite vanquish a creeping nervousness. It was also impossible for her to take her eyes from the door that must soon open on . . . what? And why were they, in effect, imprisoned? That they had been mistaken for a pair of malefactors was obvious—but supposing the members of the militia agreed with their host or, rather, their jailer?

Hard on that unsettling supposition, the earl strode to the door and called, "You . . . you've but to send to my yacht and you will have the truth of the matter."

The ensuing silence suggested that his words had fallen upon either deaf ears or no ears. He rolled his eyes at Julie and she read frustration and an increasing anger in their dark depths. Words of comfort trembled on her lips, but she did not voice them, it being a time when nothing would suffice except the illumination of their host, their subsequent release, and the hiring of men who might repair the ship. Meanwhile, time was passing and a bride was impatiently awaiting the earl, while in Brighton Lucy was also waiting for some word, if, indeed, she were still there!

The silence endured. The earl was staring moodily into space, and Julie, managing to cast surreptitious looks at her companion, saw frustration in the creases of his forehead and in the frown that lodged between his winged brows. Still, she was struck once more by that most felicitous arrangement of features, and to while the time away, she tried to imagine herself as Diana, seeing her old playmate grown to such admirable proportions and with a countenance that combined nobility with a beauty that had nothing of the feminine about it. He possessed a visage that ought to have been painted by Sir Joshua Reynolds. Unfortunately, that artist was dead, and Romney too.

She had often wished that she might paint, and had never wished it more than at this moment, when she might have, at last, sketched his face and kept that effort as a memento of an experience that must soon come to an end. She bit down a smile as she realized that Diana had fled from her mind, a mind filled with thoughts that she must not entertain. Instead, it were better to dwell on their current situation. Oddly enough, she no longer found it threatening. Sooner or later, their jailer would discover his mistake—and there would be apologies all around.

Sounds at the door banished her thoughts, and her newly acquired complacency went with them. She glanced at the earl and found that he had risen and was standing near the portal, his face a study in anger and his fists clenched. He moved back as the door opened and their erstwhile host appeared, his expression radiating triumph. "Here they are, Sir Everard," he announced in tones that demanded congratulations.

A small, compactly built man with a shock of gray hair over a blunt-featured face, strode in. He was clad in garments of good cloth, which appeared to be new. Their cut was, however, several years behind the current styles. His boots were of fine leather but scratched, and strangers to polish. Julie guessed that he was wealthy but cared nothing for the trappings of a dandy. There was, she noted, an air of authority about him, and his eyes, small and deep blue under tufted red-gray eyebrows, were suspicious. He used them to stare at the earl and more lingeringly at herself. He appeared about to speak when Lord Aylsford, obviously rendered impatient by this silent scrutiny, said sharply, "I should like to know the reasons for these untoward actions. We came here only to obtain help for our stormracked yacht and we have been detained in this house like prisoners! I am the Earl of Aylsford and this is my cousin, Miss Carleton."

"And this, your . . . er, lordship"—their host threw a

glance at the man with him—"is Sir Everard Penhurst, justice of the peace."

The earl said coolly but less impatiently, "I am pleased to make your acquaintance, Sir Everard, and may I hope—"

He was summarily interrupted by the justice. "And I might be pleased to make yours, your . . . lordship," he said coldly, evidently resenting the fact that he was forced to look upward in addressing one who could easily give him three inches. Unknowingly, he corroborated Julie's guess as he continued, "I was told that the man we seek is tall and broad-shouldered. He is known to be dark and his features are considered striking. He is also known to dress in the height of fashion. He is generally accompanied by a young woman with fair hair and blue eyes." He glanced at Julie and his eyes widened. "She is said to be comely." He turned to their erstwhile jailer. "I would say that you have done well, Master—"

"Hold," Lord Aylsford interrupted. "If you are suggesting that Miss Carleton and I are . . . wanted for any misdemeanor, I must assure you that you are in error. I am on my way to Helston to be married. My future father-in-law is Sir Nigel Penrose. However, that is aside from the point. If you wish to verify my account, my ship, the *Diana*, is anchored a short distance from your harbor. I suggest that you send one of your men out to her—my first mate, Mr. Champley, will furnish the necessary verification of our identities."

Sir Everard was silent a moment, his small eyes narrowed, his expression bordering on the pugnacious. Finally he said gruffly, "I think we owe it to the uh . . . earl at least to seek corroboration."

"I thank you, Sir Everard." The earl bowed.

He received a kindling glance from which suspicion was not yet exorcised. "I did not say that I was

convinced that you were telling the truth," Sir Everard
rasped. "But if you are not, we will know soon enough.
Meanwhile, you will remain here until we have
concluded our investigations."

"We are content with that, Sir Everard," the earl
replied calmly.

"That is well, considering that you have no choice,"
the latter said gruffly.

"More wine, more wine, come, come, come, 'tis
French and old. There's nothing like old wine unless it
be older brandy, and that you'll be having too." Sir
Everard beamed, his small eyes darting from the earl's
face to Julie's.

He sat at the head of a table too large and too long for
only three people and much too long for the lone
widower that the justice of the peace had sadly proclaimed himself to be. Probably he would not have
entertained them in so vast a hall were he not
determined to make up for the slight suffered by Lord
Aylsford and herself, Julie decided.

She thought of their would-be jailer, Mr. Madron,
with an amusement laced by pity. He had been so sure
that he had been the one to capture the pair of
miscreants who had been appearing at one door or
another in this and several other small, isolated villages
for the last several months. According to Sir Everard,
they presented themselves as either lost or shipwrecked
victims of a robbery. In this guise, the couple had
wormed their way into many a household, remaining
long enough to ascertain entrances and exits and
whether or not the place was worth robbing. Subsequently they had been followed by a villainous gang
who had robbed and, occasionally, killed at the
direction of the erstwhile guests.

Consequently Mr. Madron, setting eyes on Julie and

the earl, had been positive that he must be confronting that very pair. He had relinquished his guise of hero with the most abject apologies. Their host, too, had been similarly embarrassed. He had forthwith dispatched men to help repair the disabled vessel, and, the damage proving more extensive than Lord Aylsford had realized, Sir Everard had insisted that they be his guests for the night.

As befitted the so-called lord of the manor, Sir Everard's house was large and located on a spread of ground some little distance from the harbor. It stood on a rise and commanded a view of the sea. Tall trees protected it from the sea winds, and there was an extensive garden to the rear. The rooms were large and furnished with sturdy if not particularly elegant pieces.

Julie had already been shown her room, a very pleasant chamber once occupied, her host had explained with a touch of melancholy, by his wife, dead these three years. The bed, an immense four-poster, carved with seashells and improbable fish, had looked most inviting, and she truly wished that she might retire to it, even though it was no more than seven in the evening. Though their imprisonment had lasted less than two hours, it had told on her nerves. Furthermore, she did not quite like Sir Everard. His manner toward her bordered on the overfamiliar, and the look in his eyes brought back unwelcome memories of Mr. Travers. However, immediately that thought crossed her mind, she hastily assured herself that she was being ridiculous. One could not couple a man of her host's breeding and position with the likes of Mr. Travers! If Sir Everard seemed overly attentive, he was probably trying to atone for his earlier suspicions. Still, she would be exceedingly glad when the evening ended and she was relieved of the company of both gentlemen.

A small sigh followed this particular wish. During the

time when the earl, in common with Sir Everard, was overseeing the repairs of his yacht, she had been ensconced in the library in his house. Her host owned a large collection of volumes, many of which were very old and which, at another time, must have fascinated her. Unfortunately, and much to her chagrin, she had been quite unable to concentrate on any of them. She had actively missed the earl and had wished . . . But she did not want to dwell on those wishes at this particular moment, with Lord Aylsford sitting directly across from her, his presence activating a set of reactions that she was hard put to understand.

"And are you looking forward to visiting Helston, Miss Carleton?" Sir Everard inquired.

"Helston?" Julie looked at him blankly. "I am not going to Helston."

"Only I am going to Helston," the earl explained. "My cousin will be returning to Brighton."

"Oh, I thought you must be a bridesmaid," Sir Everard said.

"No," Julie said quickly. "I expressed an interest in visiting Cornwall, and his . . . R-Richard was kind enough to let me sail along the coast—such a beautiful voyage." She felt a warmth on her cheeks and hoped that their host had not caught her near-slip of the tongue.

"Yes, we pride ourselves on the beauty of our coast." Sir Everard smiled. "Such a voyage is, however, not without peril, as I fear you have learned."

"I have not minded the peril," Julie said softly. "It has been an adventure I shall not soon forget." She glanced at the earl. "I am most grateful to my cousin."

"The gratitude is on my side, Julie," the earl responded. "This voyage would have been tedious indeed without your company."

"Tedious, my lord? And you on the way to meet your

promised bride?'' Sir Everard gave him a quizzical look.

"But my bride was not with me, and my cousin and I have always been the greatest of friends."

"Then surely she ought to be a guest at your wedding." Sir Everard appeared surprised.

"It is not possible for me to attend," Julie said. "I had only this short time. My sister was able to relieve me at the bedside of my mother."

"I hope that your mother is not very ill," Sir Everard said sympathetically.

"She . . . has suffered at attack of apoplexy, sir," Julie improvised. Warming to her subject, she continued, "For a while we believed that she must die—but fortunately, she has rallied, else I never could have left her."

"I am glad to hear it. Aged parents can be a problem," Sir Everard said. "You have my sympathies, my dear Miss Carleton."

"It is not a problem I regret, Sir Everard," Julie assured him earnestly. "I will be glad to see my mother again, now that I have said farewell to Richard." She had, she realized, actually conjured up the image of a mother—or what a mother ought to be, and as perhaps her own mother had been to her older siblings. For a moment she had believed in her, believed, too, that she was the earl's cousin . . . No, not his cousin. She felt closer than that. A sister? No. She decided not to pursue that particular line of reasoning. However, hard on it was a desire to forsake her present company and to be alone in her borrowed chamber.

Would her host think it odd were she to excuse herself? No, it had been a difficult day. Certainly he could understand that. The earl would also understand. She put her hand up to her mouth, blinked, and said, "Oh, I am excessively weary. Would you mind if I retire now?"

"Of course not," the earl said quickly. "You have had a very tiring day, my dear."

"One for which I fear I am partially responsible," Sir Everard said gruffly. "I will have Martha show you the way, and she can act as your abigail."

"I thank you, Sir Everard," she said gratefully.

Martha, a small, slatternly woman, lighted Julie to a commodious chamber. She was gratified to find the bed turned down and a nightdress laid out for her. It was large and long, but still it would serve. There was a silver-backed brush on the dressing table. The sight of it reminded her of Lucy, who was wont to brush her hair the requisite one hundred strokes each night, even now when it was no more than shoulder length.

As Lucy undressed her, they would talk of all the little incidents that had taken place in the day. Indeed, the girl had been her one confidante. She could speak to her about matters she could not discuss with her father. Had she a woman friend . . . But she had not, and Lucy had more than sufficed. She missed the girl now as Martha helped her out of her gown. She worked capably but she was silent and rather sullen. Certainly she was no one in whom Julie could confide. Still, that was just as well, for she might have been minded to speak about the earl, to discuss his appearance, his kindness, his charm, and the strange way he made her feel—and how even that frightening time when they had been in Mr. Madron's chamber had been rendered less frightening by his presence, less frightening, and if the truth were to be told, she had been actually glad to be alone with him —because in the long days when she would no longer be able to see him, it would be something to remember and cherish.

"I'll be biddin' ye good night, ma'am," the girl said.

"Good night, Martha, and thank you," Julie said, her thoughts immediately reverting to the earl. She sighed, wishing she might be with him just a little longer—but now that the repairs were almost finished, they would be arriving in Truro very soon. The earl had assured her of that.

"You will go by stage—at least part of the way to Brighton. I think you've had enough sailing for the present."

She could never have enough, were she to sail with him, she knew, and was amazed at the sensations that were currently accompanying her thoughts. Her heart seemed to be beating faster and there was a throbbing in her throat as well as other parts of her body. There was also a need, more than a mere need, there was a strong desire to be with him. She sighed, "Oh, God, were I . . . Diana," and in that moment knew, to her sorrow, the entire meaning of love.

"I love him," she whispered incredulously, and knew, also, a despair that was deeper than any she had ever experienced. The despair had a name, and again, the name was Diana.

"I cannot think of her . . . I cannot think of him," she whispered.

There had been a time when Julie, at the urging of her nurse, had knelt to say her prayers each night before going to sleep. It had been a practice she had abandoned once her nurse had left her. Now, tossing restlessly on her pillows, she actually prayed for sleep—a sleep that would blot out this new agony and prepare her to face the following day with equanimity and with no hint of these new feelings apparent in her manner, these dangerous feelings that must never be revealed!

She blew out her candle and lay watching the long twilight of summer fade into darkness. She had hoped that the exigencies of the day would have hastened sleep, but it was a long time before she finally slept.

Julie awoke with a start and blinked against a bright,

wavering light. There was a voice in her ears, a voice that had roused her. "I thought I heard you cry out."

Julie, blinking against the light, saw that it was being held by a short figure in a long white nightshirt. "What . . . ?" she murmured.

"You cried out. I heard you. What frightened you, my dear?"

Julie, fully awake now, recognized her host. "No, I have been asleep," she said.

"Then perhaps you were having a nightmare," he hazarded.

"I . . . N-no, I am quite all right, s-sir. I thank you for your . . . solicitousness, but you need not have troubled yourself."

"It was no trouble, none at all," Sir Everard said smoothly. "I am, however, very sorry to have roused you from your . . . er . . . beauty sleep."

The flame from his candle was reflected in his eyes and Julie found the sight particularly unnerving, especially now, when the mists of sleep were dissipating and she was aware that, given the thick walls of her chamber, he could never have heard the cry he had mentioned. Striving for a calm she was far from feeling, she said, "It is of little moment, Sir Everard. I am grateful for your solicitousness, but I think I must try to go back to sleep. My cousin and I have a long day ahead of us tomorrow."

"Your . . . cousin?" He smiled. "But he is not your cousin, is he, my dear? That was obvious enough at table."

She stiffened. "I do not know what you mean, sir— and I think you had best leave my room—at once."

"But it is not precisely *your* room, my dear. It is mine. This house is mine, and all that lies within it."

Striving to conceal her rising panic, Julie said coldly, "Does that include your guests, Sir Everard?"

"It includes those who come here with lies on their lovely lips. You are no kin to the earl, my dear. You are his light of love and, indeed, I thought to find him here —but since he is not, perhaps I will suffice?"

Julie rolled swiftly away from him and slid off the far side of the bed. "If you do not leave this room, I will scream!" she said in a low, threatening tone of voice.

He laughed. "Come . . . surely you can share some of your bounty with me, my dear. And I might mention that the walls are thick and your screams will not be heard."

She glared at him. "Yet you say you heard me cry?"

His laughter was low and ugly. "I lied, my dear."

In a near-panic, Julie looked around the darkened room, hoping against hope for some means of eluding him. Then, behind her she saw a door she had not noticed when she went to bed. She moved to it hastily and was about to seize the knob when Sir Everard, coming around the bed, confronted her. "That door is locked, my sweet doxy. Come, come, come, no more of your games. How much gold does your lover shower on you? I can match him coin for coin. . . ." Purposefully he set his candle on a small table between the windows.

Julie shuddered. She was caught between the bed and the door, with Sir Everard blocking her way. In another moment he would be upon her, and his intent was in his tone and in the hard look she had glimpsed in his eyes. She was suddenly reminded of her wedding night. Her husband had looked at her with that same cold stare and had come upon her in much the same way, forcing her into bed and ravishing her. It could not happen again, no, no, not again, that tearing agony! But there was none to prevent it!

Hardly aware of what she was doing, she shrank back against the wall, crying, "Richard, Richard, Richard."

Her pursuer laughed. "Your lover cannot come to

your aid, my dear. I took the precaution of assigning him a chamber on the far side of the corridor." He sprang forward, seizing her by the shoulders, and in that same moment the bedroom door slammed back and Lord Aylsford stood on the threshold. "What is the meaning of this!" he demanded furiously.

"What . . . what are you doing in here?" Sir Everard's hands dropped to his sides.

"I would rather hear what you are doing in my cousin's chamber!" Lord Aylsford advanced into the room.

"Your c-cousin?" Their host spoke shakily, but still there was a sneer in the tone with which he added, "She's no k-kin to you, I'll wager. Share'n share alike, I say!"

"And here's my answer!" Advancing on him, Lord Aylsford struck him heavily on the chin, sending him unconscious to the floor. Hurrying to Julie's side, he put his arm around her, saying anxiously, "Did . . . he molest you, my dear?"

"No." She shuddered. "But . . . but thank God you came when you did."

"Damn him, I suspected he had something of the sort in mind. His conversation after you left the table . . . I was hard put not to strike him."

"How did you know where I was?"

"I did not know. I have been patrolling the corridor. I suspected, but I did not see him enter this room. It was a young woman, a servant, who told me to come . . . she muttered something about the master. She seemed extremely agitated and, I thought, angry. She might have been . . . But never mind that. She pointed out your door, and as I reached it, I heard you scream."

"It might have been Martha . . ." Julie said.

"Whoever it was, I am damned grateful to her. But enough. We must go."

"I know. I will dress."

"And I will see to what passes for 'justice' in these parts." Lord Aylsford lifted the unconscious man with an ease that startled Julie and carried him out of the room. In another few minutes she heard his footsteps going down the hall.

As she dressed, Julie found to her annoyance that the process presented a real problem if one was in a hurry. She had never realized there were so many small pesky buttons to be eased into holes that seemed even smaller. Furthermore, her gown buttoned down the back, and at this moment her fingers seemed to be all thumbs. Finally she had managed most of them, and having an idea that she had taken far too long, she let the others go and flung her cloak over her shoulders. Coming into the hall, she was glad to find it partially lighted by a spar of moonlight coming through a tall window at the head of the stairs. The earl was standing just beyond her door. He did not chide her, but there was a note of impatience in his tone as, cutting short her whispered apology, he said merely, "Let us hurry."

They went down the stairs as quickly as they might, given the dearth of light, and had reached the ground floor when, of a sudden, there were shapes in the darkness around them—shapes illuminated by the light of a single lantern, a glow which, to Julie's horror, revealed the swollen, angry face of their erstwhile host!

With a little cry she shrank back against Lord Aylsford, and in that same moment felt herself pulled away by one of the men. An instant later her arms were pinioned behind her back. To her horror, her captor wound a stout cord around both wrists, tying it tightly.

"Damn you, let me go," Lord Aylsford rasped as his arms, too, were similarly pinioned and bound.

"Aye, we'll let you go, my lord." Sir Everard spoke thickly through swollen lips. "Did you think you had me fast?'' he added mockingly. "There's more than one entrance to the chambers here. But 'tis knowledge that will profit neither you nor your accomplice. Come morning, you'll be put where we should have taken you ere now—to jail.''

"On what grounds—that I protected my cousin from being ravished by your . . . er . . . worship?" Lord Aylsford demanded caustically.

"Stow yer gab," his captor muttered.

"On the grounds," Sir Everard intoned, "that you did attack me without provocation and that I caught you signaling to someone from my windows. You, sir, you and your wench are the pair we have been seeking.''

"You will be laughed out of court!" Lord Aylsford retorted. "You have had corroboration from my men as to my identity, and you know, too, that this young lady is my cousin!"

"I have had corroboration, as you are pleased to put it, from a band of smugglers, who will be captured and arraigned tomorrow with your fine lordship and his bit o' muslin. You will remain in custody, the lot of you, until the assizes meet in August.''

"You will see, damn you, that the law is on my side!" Lord Aylsford said evenly.

"On the contrary, you, whoever you are, I am the law here, which you will discover when you are brought before me tomorrow morning.''

It was a boast which, in other circumstances, would have seemed as ridiculous as this posturing little man himself, Julie thought, and trembled because he was the law and they were at his mercy. A long shuddering sigh escaped her and in that same moment Lord Aylsford said icily, "I am not without influence, Sir Everard, and if you hold us without provocation—''

"Without provocation!" Sir Everard interrupted. "You've near broken my jaw. But enough! Take them to the gatehouse. They can remain there until morning. It might not be as comfortable as my apartments upstairs, my . . . lord, but I think you will find it preferable to the lodgings you will be occupying in the weeks to come."

The gatehouse, built in the shape of a small stone castle, had obviously not been used in a long time. Evidently, Julie reasoned, Sir Everard had not felt the need for a gatekeeper. As one of the two men who had escorted them to their temporary prison opened the door, she heard an ominous squeaking and by the light of their lanterns saw several small dark shapes skittering across the floor.

"Rats!" she whispered with a shudder she could not control.

"Aye," said the man beside her. "We'd best leave the light here 'neath the window, else they might grow bold'n hurt the young lady."

"Damn him!" the earl said explosively. "He knows full well we're not the pair he seeks."

"Mayhap you're not." The other man nodded. In solemn tones he continued, "An' if you're not, the truth'll out. Thass what the good book says."

"The good book'll not unbind our hands," Lord Aylsford retorted caustically. "And since you are a good Christian, will you leave us here trussed like geese ready for the market?"

"We haven't the choice, sir. He be justice o' the peace." The man spoke regretfully. "But we'll pray for ye, we will. Meanwhile, sit ye here against this wall. 'Twill be more comfortable. And all might be better in the morning, sir."

With apparent regret the two men helped Julie to sit on a bench pushed against the wall and then helped the earl to sit beside her. " 'Tis a warm night, sir," one of them said, "an' 'tis no more'n three hours afore dawn. Ye've not long to wait."

"Aye," his companion agreed. "Ye'll not be uncomfortable. Last time anyone was locked in here, 'twas the dead o' winter. They was well-nigh froze in the morning. But if yer cold, ye can sit close to each other. 'Tisn't our doin' this . . . an' we wish you well."

"Aye, that we do," sighed the other man. They went out slowly and, it seemed to Julie, still regretfully. She had a feeling that lingering in the air behind them was much they had wanted to say and even do, were they not in the employ of the justice of the peace.

She said, "Sir Everard is neither just nor peaceful."

The earl uttered a crack of shaky laughter. "When will you cease to surprise me?" he demanded.

"Have I surprised you before?" Julie inquired.

"I have ceased to count the times." He strained futilely against his bonds. "Are your hands numb, my dear?"

"Yes," Julie admitted, "but they do not trouble me. I expect your hands are numb too." Before he could answer, she added regretfully, "It was the buttons. I am sorry for that."

"The . . . buttons?" he asked confusedly.

"My abigail's in Brighton, you see. And I could not manage them . . . she manipulates them so quickly. In seconds, really. I was all thumbs!"

"I had not taken that into account. However, I had taken into account your fear and confusion at this most untoward invasion! I did not expect you to emerge as quickly as you did. And you must not apologize to me, my poor girl." Anger edged his tones. "How can you give me these apologies after an experience such as you have sustained?"

"But it was at an end," she said reasonably.

"It . . . was . . . at . . . an . . . end," he said slowly and amazedly. "You could dismiss it so quickly?"

"It does not do to brood on what you cannot mend," Julie said. "I learned that lesson early in life."

"You learned it far too early," he said in a hard voice. "Oh God," he groaned. "I cannot even put my arm around you to keep you warm."

She was startled by his sudden digression, but she was also touched. "You are kind."

"And you . . ." He hesitated. "You are quite, quite out of the ordinary, Julie. You know we are in danger, do you not? And yet . . ."

"I do not feel as if we are in danger," she said thoughtfully. "I think that the morning must bring our freedom."

"Are you an oracle, ma'am?" he asked in a tone he tried to keep light.

"Not generally," she admitted. "But we have done nothing wrong, and truth, I think, must prevail." She spoke with a certainty she barely understood herself, but quite suddenly what had been mainly reassurance had become, she was positive, a fact.

"Do you know, my dear Julie," he said softly, "that you have made me believe it too?"

The men came early the following morning. Julie heard their voices as in a dream and then felt the shoulder on which she had, at his invitation, put her head, tense. She moved back. Outside, there was laughter, rough laughter that frightened her, creeping as it had into her slumbering mind and reactivating the fears she thought she had put aside.

"My dear," the earl whispered, "believe in what you told me last night."

Even as he spoke, the door was pulled open and two men entered. They were carrying knives and in no more than a matter of minutes they had slashed the ropes that bound Sir Everard's prisoners. Then, as they rubbed Julie's wrists and the earl's as well, they told them that the guilty pair had been taken and that they were free to leave.

"Oh, Julie," Lord Aylsford said brokenly. He said no more, for there were other men confronting them as they were helped out of the gatehouse. Apologies, some abject, others gruff, filled their ears, and a Mr. Poldragon, who called himself Sir Everard's second in command, hurried them to his house for a warm breakfast and a place to rest until the repairs to the vessel were completed. Midmorning, they were rowed out to the yacht and within a matter of a few hours were bound for Truro.

6

*T*ruro.

They had reached the small but flourishing town less than a day after they left that village which had a name, but one that Julie, now standing at the window of the Red Lion, preferred to forget. The stagecoach to St. Austell had just arrived and the earl had gone to procure her a seat. From St. Austell she would go to . . . She banished the name of her destination from her mind, all the names, all the towns between here and Brighton. Each of them would take her farther and farther away from the man whose presence had added a whole new dimension to her circumscribed existence! It would not be easy to forget him . . . she would never forget him, she knew.

Until she had met Lord Aylsford, she had never known the heady excitement of a love that carried within it the seeds of passion. More than mere seeds. Planted in the rich soil of her mind and heart, they had sprouted and flourished, and now they must wither for lack of further cultivation, for soon he would be gone. Soon, soon, soon he would be on his way to Diana, the name emblazoned on the prow of his boat if not in his heart. He could hardly love someone he barely remembered. Still, he would come to love her in time—he would consider it his duty.

Duty was important to him; she knew him well enough for that. It was particularly important because, as he had so often hinted, he had neglected it in his pursuit of the pleasures London and many country houses had to offer. He had dubbed himself a rake, but certainly he did not deserve to be branded by all that term implied!

Sir James Massinger was a rake. She tried to conjure up an image of him, but she was unsuccessful. All she could see on that dark canvas back of her eyes were the features of Lord Aylsford, features she could never, never erase from her consciousness, and now, for the first time, the matter of her own disgrace sat heavily upon her heart and mind.

If only she had met him years ago—but it was futile to wish for what never could have taken place. Not only had they been born counties and years apart, her fate had been sealed practically at birth, and furthermore, the wild young man he had proclaimed himself to be must have had scant interest in the shy child she had been at seventeen. Nor did he have that interest in her now. Despite his great kindness, despite the dangers they had shared, dangers which had certainly brought them closer together, his mind was still fixed on the neglected duties of his past. He was eager to atone for them, and part of that atonement was to enter into this marriage arranged by his parents long ago.

She started. The sound of a horn was in her ears, the coachman's horn, announcing that the coach was soon to leave. She looked out and saw its brightly painted exterior, its eight restless horses, its piles of luggage, and the outside passengers on the roof. Oddly, her vision seemed to be darkened, but of course, she reminded herself, she was wearing the black veil which, with her black garments, proclaimed her a widow. The earl had insisted on this disguise. He had bought three lengths of cloth at a local dry-goods shop. All were black—two were of bombazine and a third was silk. She had protested the expense, saying that she needed but one gown—not three.

He had said masterfully, "You will need a change and it might be that you will have to dress for dinner when you change from coach to ship."

"That is highly unlikely," she had protested. He had refused to heed her protests. "One must be prepared for all emergencies," he had insisted.

He had hired a seamstress who had completed the ensembles in less than two days. While they waited for the gowns to be finished, they walked around the town, visiting St. Mary's church, which had been built during the reign of Henry VII. He told her about the tin mines in the district, explaining that Truro was the center for this flourishing industry. She could not remember much of what he told her—she had listened mainly to the sound of that voice which had first pierced her consciousness when she had thought herself dying.

"My dear . . ." He had come to stand beside her again.

Julie started. "It is time, is it not?" she asked tensely.

"Yes. I have managed to secure a place by the window for you." He stared down at her almost sternly. "I must adjure you, do not lift your veil. Remember that you are a widow in deep mourning."

"I will follow your instructions," she said dutifully.

"You must," he said urgently. "I wish I had the time to take you all the way to Brighton."

"You have done enough," she said warmly. "Were it not for you, I should be at the bottom of the sea."

"No!" he exclaimed. His voice deepened as he added, "The fates would never have been so cruel, my dear." He paused, staring at her, and then said quickly, "But come." He took her arm. As they came out of the inn and walked toward the coach, a gust of wind lifted Julie's veil, and as she hastily adjusted it, she met the interested gaze of a young man standing by the vehicle.

"You must keep that veil in place," the earl admonished her.

"It was the wind . . ." she apologized.

"Beware the wind and all the elements," he warned. "And once you are back in Brighton, I do not want you to go walking without your abigail in attendance. Indeed, you should have one with you now. . . ."

"I will be careful," she assured him.

They were nearing the coach, but the earl stopped and said almost sternly, "You have my direction in Cornwall. You will please write and tell me that you have arrived safely."

"I will, of course I will," she assured him, thinking ruefully that a letter from her would mean very little once the preparations for his wedding were under way.

All too quickly the coachman announced that the passengers must take their seats. The earl started to escort her toward the door, then suddenly bent, and lifting her veil, kissed her on the cheek, saying huskily, "Goodbye, my dear. We must not lose touch with each other. Let me know how you are doing from time to time."

"I will." She smiled mistily up at him, knowing that she would not. Then, as he handed her in, she had to add, "I will never, never forget your great kindness to me, my lord."

"I am not 'my lord' to you, Julie," he reproved. "And it is as Richard that you must address me when you write—and you must write."

"I will," she lied. "I will, Richard," she said, compounding the untruth, and was inside.

The young man she had noticed before was next to her, sitting too close for comfort, closer than he had to sit, but she could not think of that, but must needs strain to see the earl as he came around to her window to wave as the equipage started up. She waved back, waved at the man now framed in a nimbus of tears—waved until she could see him no more.

He stood watching until the coach had rumbled out of sight. There was a heaviness in his chest and an obstruction in his throat. He swallowed convulsively, but it did not go away. He defined it as fear, fear that she would not keep that veil down over her face. He had a deep-rooted belief that she had donned it only to please him, not because she believed it necessary.

"She must wear it," he found himself saying out loud, and remembered the young man he had seen standing by the coach—an inside passenger. Because of him, because of all the young men she must needs encounter on her journey back to Brighton, she must wear it! Yet would she? She was so unaware . . . so innocent.

Innocent?

Into his mind came her words, her outrageous confession—but not outrageous on her lips. *"I have no reputation."*

With that artless admission she had exposed herself to him, had given him, as it were, *carte blanche* to do as he pleased with her while she remained aboard his yacht—if he had been so minded. Perhaps he might have been if Diana had not stood between them. Diana, his bride-to-be whom he hardly remembered. Diana, who, in the few days he had been with Julie, had faded into nothingness.

He shivered, feeling a coldness in his heart and an emptiness as well. It occurred to him that he had formed a real friendship with Julie. He had never known a woman who had wanted to be his friend, who was content to be his friend. They were all full of little tricks . . . He could not dwell on the women he had known; he must concentrate on Julie, enchanting Julie—an innocent enchantress, though. She had no notion of her power to charm and delight. She seemed to imagine that her divorce had made her an outcast.

No, it was not mere imagination. In the eyes of society, she was an outcast. As had happened several times in the course of his burgeoning acquaintance with Julie, the unjustness of her position smote him again. He did remember the scandal, and mainly because he knew one of its principals.

"Sir James Massinger, damn him to perdition," he muttered.

In his mind's eye he conjured up an image of Massinger, tall, handsome, and definitely dissolute. He had met him on first arriving in London. Their acquaintance had been brief—mainly because once he began to know his way about the town, he realized that Massinger was, if not an ivory-turner, one who could easily lead an unwary young man like himself astray. He had lost several hundred pounds to one of the hells Massinger had praised, but he had no time to think of that—he had to remember that night when Massinger, in his cups, had told him a tale which he had described as highly humorous and as having a happy ending, "at least for my friend Fitzroy and the present company, who received a little something for his pains." It had, of course, concerned the part he had played in the so-called seduction of the former's unwanted young wife.

"Edwin married the chit for her money. A Season in London had left him sadly in need of the ready, and when he applied to his mama, the old dragon reminded him that he had been promised in marriage to the Carleton wench. Consequently he agreed to take unto his bosom her dowry and herself. Meanwhile, he was mad for Mark's sister, you know her, a pretty creature but without a feather to fly with. So our Edwin evolved a little plan . . ."

Massinger had gone on to describe the evening. He had laughed as he explained how he laced Lady Fitzroy's champagne with gin while she was "oohing and aahing" over the doings on the floor below her box. "She never knew how much she was imbibing, poor little mite. I vow I was quite sorry for her at the hearing. She had no notion what had happened, none at all."

"And you did not take advantage of the lady?" he had asked.

"How could I?" Sir James had demanded reasonably. "She might have been a cold corpse for all the response she made. I put her in my bed and brought her home in the morning."

He remembered having been affronted by Massinger's ensuing laughter. "And what happened to the girl?" he had asked.

"God knows!" Massinger had shrugged dismissively. "She was divorced, of course, and Edwin petitioned to keep the dowry. Her parents consented."

"And she was disgraced, of course. Wasn't that rather hard on the poor child?"

Massinger had had the grace to look ashamed. "I expect it was . . . but she was such a plain little thing . . . no, not actually plain, but so quiet, not an ounce of charm . . . anyhow, all is well that ends well. Our Edwin has the dowry and the wife of his heart."

And poor Julie had suffered ostracism, had been locked away in the country for eight years, she, the victim, forced to wear the mask of villiany. His face darkened. If he had Sir Edwin here . . . But he had not to dwell on that. He must concentrate on artless Julie, living on her sequestered estate with only her father as companion. She knew nothing of the world . . . At that moment an image sprang into his mind. He saw that young man in the coach. He had seen her veil wind-caught, had looked upon her face!

The earl grimaced. He had a moment of wishing that

Julie were a Mohammedan maiden, her face always
veiled whenever she ventured abroad, but he was being
foolish! She was not a Mohammedan and she was so
very vulnerable. She never should have gone off alone
in that stagecoach! And she would also have to book
passage on a ship . . . would she be able to manage that
by herself? She ought not to be by herself. It was a long
journey and she was no more up to snuff than . . .

"I was mad!" he groaned. Almost without volition,
he strode back to the inn to settle the bill. In a few more
minutes he was hurrying down the river where his yacht
lay at anchor.

"We'll be suppin' at the White 'Orse Inn," Mr.
Claude Payne was saying to Julie. "May I 'ope you'll be
my guest, miss? What is your name, my dear?"

"That is no concern of yours, sir," Julie said coldly.
"And I would prefer if you did not sit so close to me.
Surely that is not necessary."

"Ah, you're a feisty little piece, ain't you?" Mr.
Payne observed. "I like a female with spirit, I do."

Julie sighed and kept her eyes trained on the passing
scenery. She wished that she were sitting beside the thin
clergyman across from her or next to a thin young
woman who was staring almost desperately out of the
window. The other passenger, across the way, the
clergyman's mousy little wife, would also be preferable
to Mr. Payne, and nor would she have minded sitting
next to the heavyset woman on her side. She moved
nearer to the coach door—but that availed her nothing.
Mr. Payne's knee remained pressed against her knee
and he was continuing to speak to her, his voice low and
insinuating. She wanted to think about the earl, but it
was impossible to concentrate when the man beside her
kept up his steady stream of fulsome compliments.

"Can you not see that you are annoying the lady?" the clergyman said.

Julie shot him a grateful look at the same time that Mr. Payne, glaring at her defender, growled, "What's it to you, you horse-faced old—"

"Shame on you!" the heavyset woman in the corner exclaimed. "The idea . . . speakin' to a clergyman like that."

" 'Tweren't me wot spoke first!" retorted Mr. Payne sulkily. However, he put his head back against the squabs and closed his eyes.

He was still sitting far too close to her, but at least he was no longer speaking to her, and that was a mercy! Julie restrained a strong impulse to dig him in the ribs with her elbow. Given his obviously high opinions of himself and his charms, it was quite possible that he would consider it a familiarity rather than a rebuff. She could not understand his persistence. She had given him no encouragement at all, and furthermore, she was supposedly a widow. What manner of individual intruded on a woman's grief? She sighed and stared out of the window at a craggy landscape. They had covered two hours of their journey, but another hour remained, and miserable as she was at the thought of the lengthening distance between herself and the earl, she would be glad when they halted and she might be free of any more attentions from the odious man beside her.

That hour crept by, and still they had not arrived at their destination. At one point they had been held up by a large flock of sheep crossing the road, and there was also a wait by a stream swollen by a recent rain, but finally, finally, they rolled into St. Austell!

"Ah, 'ere we are at last," Mr. Payne murmured. "I've 'eard as 'ow there's a most interestin' church in this 'ere town. Per'aps you'd like to visit it, ma'am."

"No, I would not," Julie said shortly.

"Maybe yer 'ungry. I could buy you a bit to eat." He grinned at her.

In her corner, the heavyset woman suddenly rasped, "Whyn't you stop hectoring the little lady. She don't want none o' your company and 'oo could blame her."

Mr. Payne glared at her. "An' why don't you mind your own business, you ill-conditioned old witch."

"Old witch, am I?" The lady glared at him. "I wish I was . . . because then I could turn you into the toad you ought to be."

"Ah, 'old yer tongue . . ." Mr. Payne glared at her.

"Out ye come!" bawled the coachman, creating a very welcome diversion for Julie. "We're 'ere for two hours . . . two hours'n ye'd best 'ave somethin' to eat."

The doors were opened and the six inside passengers climbed wearily out. The young woman who had stared so fixedly at her window moved hurriedly away. Julie had a mind to go after her and offer the words of comfort she seemed to need, but she was stopped by Mr. Payne, who caught her by the arm.

"Now, come wi' me, my dear," he said determinedly.

Julie tried to pull away, but to no avail. "Sir," she snapped, resenting her slender body and lack of inches as never before. "I do not wish to be in your company. Now let me go!"

Her would-be companion's face darkened. "If I were 'im wot brought you 'ere, you'd be singin' a different tune, I'll warrant." He snarled. "Wot's the matter with me? I'm not good enough for the likes o' a female wot's travelin' alone?" An insinuating grin displaced his snarl.

"If you do not release me," Julie said loudly, "I will scream."

"Scream away," Mr. Payne began, and came to a startled stop as in that same moment a hand descended upon his collar and jerked him back.

"Did you not hear the lady?" an irate voice demanded. "She has told you that she wishes to be relieved of your company."

Wondering if she were not having a vision, Julie looked up into the face of the earl. "Richard . . . oh, Richard," she cried.

"Lemme go," whined Mr. Payne. " 'Oo do you think you are?"

The earl did not release him. His eyes on Julie, he said, "Stay there, my dear. I will be with you presently."

Still clutching Mr. Payne's collar, the earl dragged him away, and thrusting him roughly against the wall of an adjacent building, said, "I suggest that you remove yourself immediately, else I might be minded to deal with you in a way—" Whatever else he might have uttered died on his lips as Mr. Payne, wrenching himself out of Lord Aylsford's grasp, darted away, disappearing swiftly around a corner.

The earl did not give him a second look. Striding back to Julie, he said solicitously, "I pray you took no harm of that miscreant?"

"No, no, he was only annoying," Julie assured him. "Oh, Richard, what are you doing here? Why are you not on your way to—?"

"My dear," he interrupted, "I must have been out of my mind, letting you go off alone on so long a journey. You are no more able to fend for yourself than . . . than a child. You will have to come with me to Excalibur Hall."

"Excalibur Hall?" she repeated incredulously.

A smile lighted his somber eyes. "It is the fanciful name of my future father-in-law's estate. It was not his doing, I might mention, but his father's, whose passion for the Arthurian legends that abound in Cornwall exceeded all the boundaries of common sense. He named his son Arthur, and if he had had his way, he would have called his granddaughter, Guinevere.''

Julie stared at him dazedly. His words had hardly registered. She was still thinking of his incredible demand. "I cannot come with you," she said in a low voice. "You are to be married."

"Yes," he said impatiently, "but there will be those present whom I can trust to bring you back to Brighton safely. You will have only to wait until after the ceremony."

"I do not see—" she began.

"I will hear no more arguments from you," he interrupted, adding determinedly and earnestly, "I would not have a single easy moment, knowing you were bound for Brighton alone."

"But your bride . . .''

"She will understand," he said confidently. "I will tell her that you are the widow of my best friend, Sir Christopher Winslow, who died of his wounds at Waterloo." A shadow passed over his face. "That last is true."

"I am sorry," she said.

"As am I. He was a good friend. On the way to Porthleven I shall tell you about him. I shall also explain to Sir Nigel that you were living in Brighton and I went to visit you before coming to Cornwall. I found you quite ill with grief and brought you on this voyage in the hopes of restoring your spirits. You have but to appear melancholy and I will enlarge upon this tale—making it so heartrending that they will question neither of us." He fixed a compelling stare on her face. "I will brook no arguments from you, my dear Julie. You must do as I say."

She gazed up into his stern face, and though something deep within her mind told her this was sheer madness, something else refused to allow her to protest that same madness. She said softly and with a meekness quite foreign to her, "Very well, Richard, I will come with you."

They were nearing Porthleven at last. It had taken them two full days to reach it, and Julie had ventured to chide the earl for going so far out of his way.

He had said firmly, "I had no choice, filled as I was with visions of you telling some other stranger that you were divorced and disgraced." He had added with a frown, "Have you no notion how some could take advantage of so provocative a confidence?" Without giving her a chance to reply, he had continued thoughtfully, "I think that I must bring you back to Brighton myself."

"You could not!" she had protested. "Your bride would never understand!"

"I will invent a logical reason, and meanwhile, I must remind you once more—you must stress your grief. Think of 'Niobe, all tears,' as it were."

She was mulling over the conversation in her mind as the ship docked in the small port, its pristine whiteness forming a strong contrast to the rather battered vessels nearby. These, Richard had told her, carried tin from the surrounding mines to be smelted. In the olden days, he had explained, the mines had been worked by slave labor. Hundreds of captive Jews brought from Rome had been forced underground. There were some who believed their spirits dwelt in the mines, making the strange tapping sounds that present miners insisted they heard as they labored in those same depths. Poor Jews. It must have been particularly horrible for them, coming from the sunny reaches of their own bright land and . . . But she could not dwell on ancient sorrows. They did not help to alleviate her own as she stared upward at the town of Helston, built on two hills.

Beyond Helston lay Excalibur Hall, and in it dwelt Diana Penrose, soon to be the Countess of Aylsford.

To quell a pain in her heart as she envisioned the earl's meeting with his bride, she concentrated once more on what he had told her of the surrounding countryside.

"It is supposed to be an Arthurian domain. Two miles from Helston is the Looe Pool, which, in effect, is a large freshwater lake. Supposedly Arthur's sword Excalibur lies in its depths. However"—he had smiled derisively—"there are many other places in Cornwall and in Somerset, as well, where it might also have been taken by that most elusive fairy—the Lady of the Lake. There is a Spanish galleon that was driven over a sandbar during a fearful storm in the harbor and supposedly sunk in the lake. It still attracts divers, who hope to find its gold and jewels. Too often, they have found only death. There's also a haunted castle nearby, and if that were not enough, there are the Kissing Rocks that lie on Sir Nigel's estate. There's a legend attached to them too—not a very pleasant one."

"I should like to hear it," she had said.

He had been about to tell her the tale when Mr. Champley had called him, and now they were due to dock and there would be even less time to speak with him—less time to see him. In fact, she wished almost that she were on the stagecoach or on the boat she would have ultimately taken to Brighton—but she was not. She had let her passion for him triumph over her discretion, and that had been very, very foolish. She ought never to have agreed to come with him. Yet, could she have refused? She had a distinct feeling that if she *had* refused, he would have carried her on board. And now she would be forced to see him every day they remained at Excalibur Hall. She would also be forced to attend his wedding, forced to pretend that her heart was buried in the grave with her late husband, her fictitious husband—and all the time, she would be watching him woo Diana!

How could he have wanted to put her through this agony, knowing the condition of her heart, knowing how very much she loved him?

The answer to that question was simple: he did *not* know, and she herself, though much attracted to him, had not been entirely sure of her real feelings until they were ready to part. When she had seen him again, when he had come to rescue her from that odious Mr. Payne, she had wanted to dance and sing for joy, she had wanted to throw her arms around him. Yet she had managed to keep those emotions in check, and must needs do so in the days remaining before the wedding, and, of course, afterward!

Afterward. She was suddenly very glad of her veil. She had pushed it back in order to see that hillside town more clearly, and now she brought it down to hide her face or, more specifically, her tear-filled eyes.

"If we had arrived in Helston on the eighth of May," the earl said as, seated in the post chaise he had hired in Porthleven, they neared the town in question, "we would have seen and perhaps even participated in the Furry Dance."

"The . . . Furry Dance?" Julie repeated. "Does that mean they wear fur? In May?"

"No," he laughed. "No one is quite sure about the derivation of the name—but the Furry Dance is a celebration marking a day, centuries ago, when Helston was saved from annihilation."

"Really!" Julie exclaimed. "How? Would it have been the Spaniards or the Romans?"

"Neither. It seems that the devil intended to drop a huge block of stone on the town—but an angel prevented it. Consequently, the citizens danced for joy and have been dancing ever since—at least, on the eighth of May."

"Oh"—Julie found that she, too, could laugh— "that is a delightful tale."

"It is not a mere tale, my dear," he said with mock solemnity. "It is purported to be the absolute truth. And everyone still joins in the dance. Diana and I did. So did our parents. I stamped on her foot, I remember, and she got even with me by hurling a rock at me, once we were on our way up the hill again."

"Gracious! I hope she did not hurt you!" Julie exclaimed.

"As a matter of fact, she did, rather. Actually, it frightened me more than it hurt me—it was so unexpected. It was also very sharp. It could have blinded me." He touched his eyebrow. "You can still see the scar."

Julie, leaning forward, discerned a white ridge running below his eyebrow. She shuddered and touched it lightly. "It was close!" she exclaimed. "Oh dear, I hope they punished her."

He caught her hand and kissed it lightly. "It is late for sympathy, my dear. That wound's long healed."

"I hope her capacity to bear grudges has cooled," Julie said a trifle breathlessly, wishing he would release her hand. In that same moment, he did, and conversely, she missed its warmth.

"I am sure that it has. She was only a child, after all, and I must have stamped heavily on her foot. What would you have done?"

"I expect I might have scolded you. Perhaps I might even have slapped you—but I know I would not have thrown a rock at you."

"I am sure you would not have done anything," he said thoughtfully. "Judging from everything you have told me, you seem to lack the capacity for retaliation." There was a frown in his eyes as he added, "I wish that some member of your family might have treated Sir Edwin Fitzroy as he deserved.''

She regarded him in surprise. "But everyone in my family felt so sorry for him—Mama especially.''

"The poor cuckold?" he demanded sarcastically.

"He might have been," Julie sighed. "As I have told you, I do not remember.''

"I would lay odds . . ." he began, and broke off. "You must look out of the window, my dear. There's the main street of Helston. See the narrow little streams on either side.''

"Oh!" Julie exclaimed as she gazed in the direction he was indicating. "They are so clear.''

"Yes, clear and fresh. Over there is the town church. It is nothing much in the way of architecture. It replaces, I understand, a much more beautiful building, which, unfortunately, was destroyed by lightning.''

"Gracious, the weather must be rather uncertain here," she commented.

"The weather's like much else in Cornwall—contrary and, on occasion, strange.''

"I have always heard it was a land of myth and legend, even aside from its connections with King Arthur.''

"That is true. Mermaids have supposedly sung upon these shores, and one was stranded in a nearby harbor— by the tide. Then, there is Tregeagle, who was a wicked steward, so wicked that he was eventually slaughtered by the tenants of the estate over which he presided. It was his ghost that supposedly dumped all the sand in the Porthleven harbor, making it dangerous to shipping. Furthermore, on windy nights he is seeen in a phantom coach accompanied by—''

"Oh, stop," Julie protested. "I think you are trying to frighten me.''

He smiled at her and retrieved her hand. "Acquit me of that, my dear Mrs. Winslow. I . . ." He paused and added, "Ah, here we are on the Helston road, and not far from here is Excalibur Hall."

"And your bride-to-be."

His grasp tightened. "Yes, the tempestuous Diana."

"I hope her rock-throwing days are at an end." Julie managed a little laugh.

"We will soon see." He released her hand, and turning away from her, stared out of the window.

She sensed a tension in him, and a withdrawal as well, indications, she decided, that the meeting with his bride was suddenly uppermost in his mind.

At least, she thought sympathetically, Diana was not an entirely unknown quantity, and if she had come close to blinding him, it was a child's impulse and carried no other implications, else he would not be on his way to marry her, family or no family.

She, on the other hand, had never met Edwin in the days when she was growing up, and nor, to her certain knowledge, had her brothers and sisters known those they were eventually constrained to marry. Much as she had come to love and even adore her father, she had yet resented this arbitrary coupling. Furthermore, it was not always the rule among the *ton*. Lucy, whose sister Mary was also an abigail, had told her that the family for whom Mary worked had let their children choose for themselves.

"And Mary says as 'ow their marriages turned out ever so good," had been Lucy's comment.

Julie suddenly slipped back in her seat, and a quick glance out of the window showed her that the road had grown much steeper. A few moments later they turned onto a smaller, tree-shaded lane which, fortunately, leveled off. Halfway down the lane was a long, massive wall bisected by a high towered gate, a formidable structure made of dark weathered stones. If it had worn a face, she thought, it must have been frowning.

Quite as if he had read her mind, Richard said,

"Those are the gates of Excalibur Hall. They were erected long before the name was changed. They give the impression of a fortress rather than a house, do you not agree?"

"I do." She nodded, repressing a little shiver. "But I expect they must have been built when such protection was needed."

"That's true. The house, if I remember correctly, is quite pleasant, though, again, it might not look it. And though many an ancient manor house in these parts is supposedly haunted, there are no ghosts at Excalibur Hall, and there are some very lovely gardens. However, down the road there is a ruined castle which rejoices in some very restless spirits."

"I am not sure I believe you." Julie smiled.

He smiled back. "Do you not? Good, I do not believe in them either. However, Diana might. She led me there one day . . ." He laughed. "I'd almost forgotten about that. We climbed over—or under—a broken gate. I am not quite sure which, and we came into a dusty hall . . . there was a long broken staircase and cobwebs at all the windows. It smelled of bats and rats. Diana said, '*They* come here at midnight.' "

"Who were *they*?"

"According to Diana, they were an unhappily married pair who fought all the time. Then one day they declared a truce and the husband reportedly said to his wife, 'Let us drink to our future happiness.' She agreed, and that night they drank and died, each having dropped poison into the other's goblet. Diana thought it very amusing. I remember her bursting into giggles and saying, 'Was it not a good joke on them!' "

"Brrrr." Julie pretended to shudder. "Children always love such tales because they have no notion of the horror behind them. But still, I beg you'll not tell me any more of these stories, else I will be quite afraid to reside in yon fortress." She managed a laugh, but

actually she felt far from laughing, because finally they
had arrived at that formidable gate and the coach
stopped so that the coachman could alert the gatekeeper
to their presence. While she did not fear bricks and
mortar, there was something behind that dark facade
that she feared far more than airy phantoms—and that
was Diana Penrose, the bride-to-be of the man she
loved.

The gate was opened by an elderly gizzled man who,
on hearing the earl identify himself, broke into a face-
splitting grin that activated deep wrinkles on either side
of his mouth. "Your lordship, I do not expect you'll be
remembering me, you being a lad when last you came
here."

"But I do, now that I see you more closely," the earl
responded heartily. "Jem, is it not?"

"Aye, Jem, it is." The gatekeeper grinned even more
widely.

"And it was you who first showed me the pool . . ."

"I did . . . and you were all for diving down to find
the sword." The old man laughed.

Lord Aylsford laughed too. "I also wanted to see the
Lady of the Lake. And you told me she would be
keeping it safe until King Arthur arose to defend
England again."

"Aye, it's a good memory you have," Jem said.

"Jem, here, is an authority on the subject of King
Arthur," the earl explained to Julie.

"I shall want to see that fabled lake," Julie said, and
flushed as she met the old man's frankly appraising
stare.

The earl must have seen it too, for he said quickly,
"This is Mrs. Winslow, Jem. And this, Julie, is Jem,
who used to take me fishing on that lake."

"I am glad to meet you, sir," Julie said shyly.

"And I, you, ma'am." The gatekeeper's gaze had
become quizzical.

"Mrs. Winslow is newly widowed. Her husband, Christopher, was my best friend. He was killed at Waterloo. And she is on her way to Brighton to stay with her cousin, or will be, after the wedding."

"Oh, 'tis sorry I am, Mrs. Winslow," the gatekeeper said with a commiserating look, "and you so young. Too many died at Waterloo, they did. Too many."

"Yes," Julie sighed, glad that the gatekeeper's sympathy was collective rather than specific. The horror of Waterloo still lingered and she could feel less guilty about the lie that Richard had offered so glibly.

" 'Tis well the monster's confined once more, and let us hope he'll be staying where they put him this time," Jem growled. "But enough, I'll send my son to let the master know you're comin', my lord."

"I beg you'll not be so formal, Jem. Am I not still Richard to you?"

The gatekeeper's smile appeared again. "If you'll have it thus, Richard, my lad."

"I will have it thus." The earl smiled and ordered the coachman to move on.

The meeting seemed to have pleased Richard, Julie noted. There was almost a boyish exuberance about him as he said, "Jem's a good man. And there's nothing he does not know about the countryside and its tales. He used to keep my hair on end with his stories of witches, piskies, enchanted hares, and, worse yet, for they were real, smugglers and wreckers."

"He seems very fond of you," she remarked.

"Yes . . . he was like a father to me when I was first here. My own father was considerably older than I . . . forty-one when he was wed, and he had not much patience with children. It was Jem who, in his spare time, taught me woodcraft, but . . ." He paused as the coach slowed down. "I think we must be near the house and—"

"Your bride," Julie said, and clamped her teeth

down to imprison her unruly tongue. Had she sounded as regretful and as nervous as she felt?

"Yes, Diana," the earl said. "Look, my dear, there it is. Excalibur Hall."

Leaning out of her window, Julie saw a massive house constructed of the same dark red stone she had seen at the gate. It rose three stories, though she guessed that the third floor must contain servants' quarters or possibly an attic, by reason of its small windows. On the first two levels the windows were tall and narrow. The front door was paneled, and as they drew closer, she saw that it was centered by a knocker in the shape of a lion's head. Fronting the door was a small porch reached by a double pair of stairs. She had seen many houses built on that same plan and scale. Consequently there was no reason for her to feel so intimidated by this one—but she did, and, of course, her reasons had nothing to do with the house itself.

Behind that facade, Richard's bride awaited him, and probably—undoubtedly—she was impatient and wondering what had caused his delay. When would the ceremony take place? In that moment she wished most heartily that she had not agreed to come with him—but she had not come willingly, not really. He had insisted, and she had not possessed the strength, or, if she were to be totally honest with herself, the will to refuse.

"Julie, did you hear me?"

She started, and looking at Richard, saw that the coach door was open. She had been so deep in thought that she had not even realized that the vehicle had stopped. She said confusedly, "I . . . I was thinking . . . I did not hear you."

"I said that the footman is waiting to hand you down, my dear."

She blushed, and moving to the door, quickly took the man's proffered hand as she negotiated the three steps set there for her convenience.

In a few moments they had reached the entrance and had been ushered into an immense hall with a high beamed ceiling and a huge marble fireplace flanked on either side by full suits of armor—complete with visored helmets. A frayed tapestry hung on the wall facing the fireplace, and a long wooden table was probably a reminder of the feasts that had once been eaten in what must have been the warmest room in the house. High overhead there was a minstrel's gallery.

As Julie absorbed and admired these particulars, she was also attuned to the imminent arrival of the bride-to-be and her father. However, it was only a darkly handsome middle-aged man who hurried down the flight of stairs she glimpsed through an open door. Hurrying into the hall, he had a cordial greeting for the earl, but he was evidently surprised and confused by the sight of herself.

Julie held her breath as the earl told Sir Nigel the tale they had agreed sounded the most plausible. Did it?

Would her host not wonder at the cruelty of the elderly cousin who had refused to let the poor young widow remain with her in Truro? Would he not protest the notion of Richard with his bride taking her to her friend in Brighton, the friend who had not yet arrived in the town, but would be there in another fortnight?

She was both relieved and embarrassed by the sympathy she found reflected in Sir Nigel's gaze. His eyes, she noted, were a greenish hazel, and at first she had found them singularly penetrating, as if, indeed, he could see into her mind and discover the real reason for her presence at Excalibur Hall and know, too, that the only grain of truth in the tale concerned her eventual return to Brighton.

Coming forward to lift her hand to his lips, he held it warmly as he said, "You have my very deepest sympathies, my dear Mrs. Winslow. I have had too many friends who have suffered similar losses in that terrible conflict. And you . . . I expect your loss is even greater, as you're so alone in the world.''

"I . . . I cannot think it greater, Sir Nigel, but I . . . do miss Christopher," Julie said softly, hating herself for this imposture.

"I can imagine that you would, my poor girl. I am glad that you will soon be going to stay in Brighton. It has become a very popular resort in the last few years— and there will be much to distract you from your grief. I know it is early to think of such distractions, but . . ." He paused as a tall dark young woman suddenly came in, pausing momentarily on the threshold. Then, seemingly oblivious of anyone else in the hall, she hurried to the earl, saying in a low, slightly husky voice, "But, at last you have arrived, Richard. I had begun to believe you intended to keep me waiting at the altar!"

"Diana, my dear!" Sir Nigel protested.

She did not take her gaze from the earl's face, and since she had stretched out both hands, which he had automatically grasped, it would have been difficult for her to turn away even if she so wanted. Julie, her heart plummeting, was quite sure that Miss Diana Penrose did not want to turn away from her old playmate and bride-groom-to-be.

A glance at Richard's face revealed a bemused amazement and admiration. Yes, Julie thought, he admired her, as well he might. Though the glimpse she had had of the girl as she stood poised on the threshold for a half-moment was brief, she had managed to note compelling, long-lashed green eyes set in an oval face surmounted by coils of dark, lustrous hair. And now, as Diana turned away from the earl, Julie was able to see that her brows were arched, her nose straight, and her mouth, although a little wide by the standards of the day, withal beautifully shaped. There was the suggestion of a cleft in her chin, and if these were not riches enough, her figure was excellent and she must needs be at least seven inches over five feet! Her gown, a pale green muslin, accentuated her eyes and made her look like a forest nymph or, rather, a goddess.

Julie, feeling dwarfed and diminished by this statuesque young beauty, found it very difficult to smile at her, to acknowledge her father's introduction, to accept Diana's sympathies for her briefly described plight, and to know that, in this moment, her very worst fears had been realized.

From the bemused, almost dazed look in Richard's eyes, Julie was positive that he had fallen in love at first—or, rather, second—sight, given their prior acquaintance. She also realized what she ought to have known from the very first: she should never have agreed to come here with him.

How could she manage to conceal her real feelings for even a day—much less the probable fortnight that she was to remain at the house? Then, as she pondered this problem, she heard Richard speaking about his late friend Christopher and his aborted life. In that moment she could be almost glad for the part she was playing—because widows were not expected to look happy, were they? She had come to this house clad in mourning cloth, and, she realized dolefully, it was no longer a mere disguise. She had, in a regrettably short time, lost someone she had come to love with all her heart!

7

Excalibur Hall was spacious and the rooms were large. Julie's chamber, hastily prepared by several servants under the direction of a harried housekeeper, was immense. The furniture was similarly large. In addition to its size, the bed, a wide four-poster, was, Julie guessed, of considerable antiquity. It was covered by a rose silk spread to match a canopy surmounted by a golden crown. A soft, velvety carpet was also rose-colored, and the damask curtains at the windows were rose striped with gold. The furnishings included a richly carved wardrobe and a delicate writing table that appeared to be of Italian manufacture. An ormolu clock ticked on the mantelshelf and a wide mirror reflected the chamber.

Judging from the furniture, the vases and figurines, some of Meissen and others of jade and ivory, no cost had been spared. Indeed, from what she had seen of the house, her host was undoubtedly a generous man. His daughter's dowry would be large.

She did not want to dwell on dowries. She moved to the window and was pleased to find that it overlooked the gardens. These, bathed in the afternoon sunlight, seemed vast. Directly facing her was a rose arbor, and a short distance away she saw a fish pool centered by the marble figure of a mermaid sculptured in the act of enjoying the silvery streams of water that incessantly

rose and fell about her. Julie felt an urgent desire to
examine the fountain more closely, or was that desire
more specific? She nodded. Yes, she wanted to be out of
her chamber, out of the house, and away, far, far away,
where she would not need to be in the company of the
earl and his beautiful bride-to-be as they delightedly
exchanged childhood memories, while their pleasure in
each other increased by the moment!

Unwillingly Julie summoned up an image of Diana—
hardly necessary, since she would be seeing her every
day until the wedding, and afterward if the earl insisted
on bringing her back to Brighton. Yet, having fixed
Diana's image in her mind's eye, she had perforce, to
gaze on it and be reminded of perfection. Yet, at the
same time, she had discerned a certain hardness in the
gaze that her hostess had turned on her. Was she
imagining that?

Diana had listened to the explanation of her presence
at the house with what had appeared to be sympathetic
understanding and had also voiced that sympathy. Yet
Julie had a distinct impression that the girl regarded her
with the same resentment that she herself could not help
feeling for Diana.

"Is that true?" Julie whispered, and wished that Lucy
were with her. She needed a confidante. She needed
Lucy's common sense and sympathy, but in that same
moment her own common sense emerged to tell her that
neither of these assets would have served to assuage the
pain in her heart. She had hoped, most regrettably—
she was quite aware of this—that Diana and Richard
would not be happy with each other. But what man in
his right mind would not be elated at the thought of
wedding the very personification of feminine beauty?
Had Diana been in London, the dandies would not have
hesitated to vote her an Incomparable!

Diana, in fact, stood to have a great success in

London. The beautiful Lady Aylsford would grace many a ball, and no doubt she would be a frequent visitor at Carlton House, Richard being an intimate friend of the Prince Regent. They would be a handsome couple, Lord and Lady Aylsford.

The garden blurred and Julie crossly wiped eyes that had suddenly become tear-drenched. She was being very selfish. The earl was committed to this marriage, and judging from his earlier experiences with the child Diana, he had not been entirely sanguine in his mind regarding the duty thrust upon him by his parents. However, it was now no longer needful for her to feel any kinship with him in that regard. She could compare his probable sensations to her own—had he been the bridegroom whom her mother had introduced to her.

Foolish tears blurred her vision and sobs rose to her throat. Abruptly she turned away from the window. She would go into the gardens. She moved swiftly across the wide expanse of her chamber, and in a few minutes she was outside in the sunlight. It remained only to go into the gardens and find the fountain she had seen from her window.

She had expected to reach her goal easily enough, but the denseness of the gardens amazed Julie. They were, she realized, on several levels descending down a small hill to a swift-flowing stream. There appeared to be acres of green lawn, groves of trees, and everywhere, flowers! Some were planted in patterned beds and others were seemingly allowed to grow wherever they took root, but, Julie guessed, it was an organized disorder. Forgetting her original destination, she wandered about at will, sometimes on carefully raked paths and sometimes on flagstone walks. There were, she noted, little marble benches set about in some particularly peaceful spots, and at one point, rounding a planting of roses, she happened upon a grove of cedars.

Set in the center was a Grecian statue of indisputable
antiquity and, she guessed, probably purchased in
Greece. It put her in mind of the newly arrived Elgin
Marbles. She had longed to see them, but London had
been denied to her these eight years past. She winced,
not wanting to dwell on that part of her life. Yet why
not think of it? Why not, at this melancholy moment,
remember that even were the earl to look on her as more
than a friend, her reputation must needs preclude any
closer relationship. Richard had not appeared to mind
her fall from grace . . . but why should he mind it? They
were friends and he could countenance in a friend that
which he could never accept in a wife! And why could
she even think of marriage, she, who had loathed the
experience? However, she would not loathe it were she
married to Richard, she was positive of that. He was so
kind. There had been nothing kind about Edwin, not
even at the very first. As they had driven away from the
Manor, he had scarcely spoken to her. Indeed, he had
seemed as melancholy as if he had just been present at a
funeral rather than his marriage! She had been in much
the same mood, already missing her home. She had not
been very happy there . . . but she had had a feeling of
doom . . .

"But who are you?"

Startled, Julie turned quickly and found herself
confronted by a tall young man casually dressed for the
country but in clothes that smacked of good London
tailoring. His hair was almost as fair as her own and his
eyes were gray and, again like her own, unexpectedly
framed in thick dark lashes. He had asked her a
question, she remembered.

"I am Mrs. Winslow, sir."

"Oh, you came with his highness . . ." He reddened.
"I mean, you are the widowed friend of Lord
Aylsford."

"I am, sir," Julie corroborated. "But you have the advantage of me. I do not know your identity."

"I am sorry. It is Revell, Anthony Revell." He regarded her appreciatively. "You are, indeed, young to be a widow, Mrs. Winslow."

Julie responded repressively, "My husband was young to die, sir."

A wave of red stained his face. "That was a ridiculous comment. I pray you will excuse me, Mrs. Winslow." Without giving her an opportunity to reply, he continued hastily, "It was only that I did not expect to . . . well, I did not expect that you would be so entirely lovely." His flush deepened. "But I fear I . . . I grow too familiar. May I offer you my very deepest sympathies and hope that you will excuse my maladroitness?"

"I thank you, sir, and of course you are excused." Julie decided that a slight smile would not be out of order.

"You could not have been married very long," he commented, his eyes on her face again.

She tensed. She and Richard had not discussed the length of her marriage. She said carefully, "It was not long, sir, but we had been friends since childhood."

"Ah, I understand that well enough," her companion said bitterly. "I think my situation might even parallel your own."

"Oh, did you lose someone you loved too?" Julie asked, feeling a sudden kinship with Mr. Revell.

"Not exactly, but . . ." He paused as Diana Penrose hurried into the clearing, coming to a dead stop as she saw Julie. Mr. Revell's flush deepened. "Diana . . ." he said, obviously trying to appear surprised by an arrival which, Julie guessed, was entirely expected.

Diana, on the other hand, seemed both startled and miffed. "Good afternoon, Sir Anthony," she said coolly. "I imagine it is not necessary to introduce our guest to you."

"No, we have met," he corroborated, with an effortful smile at Julie.

The tension that emanated from the pair was almost palpable, Julie thought. Glancing at Diana, she met the girl's eyes and found them chill. Diana said, "I thought you must be resting in your room, Mrs. Winslow. You did speak about being weary. I am glad to see that you have recovered so soon."

There was an ironic tinge to her speech that suggested both doubt and suspicion. Julie, however, determinedly ignored it, saying lightly, "I was indeed weary, and my recovery, I am sure, was based on the appearance of your grounds from my window. The gardens proved far too enticing to ignore. I have always been very fond of flowers. My husband and I shared that interest."

There was not so much as a flicker of sympathy in Diana's eyes as she said merely, "I see."

Sir Anthony appeared embarrassed by the girl's chill manner. He said, "It is sad that Mrs. Winslow should have been widowed so early in life."

"Yes, it is most unfortunate," Diana agreed in tones suggesting that she was entirely disinterested in any sorrows sustained by this unexpected and, Julie was sure, unwanted guest.

"I hope," she said, "that you will excuse me. As I have explained, I am fond of gardens and I am very anxious to explore these."

"Of course," Diana returned, smiling for the first time. "If you go down the hill, you will find the stream. There are fish in it—and some very tasty watercress."

"I will take your advice, thank you." Julie smiled.

"Until later, then, Mrs. Winslow," Sir Anthony said. "You must also see the lake, and perhaps I may be allowed to take you rowing?"

Julie, seeing Diana's brows draw together in a frown, bit down a smile. The young woman's jealousy was very evident, and if the truth were to be told, her own feelings were all too close to those of her hostess, her most unwelcoming and reluctant hostess. She contented herself with saying merely, "You are very kind, sir. I will bid you good afternoon."

"Good afternoon, Mrs. Winslow." His gaze lingered on her face. "I shall look forward to seeing you again."

"And I, you," Julie responded courteously, and then tensed as an inadvertent glance at Diana revealed an even deeper frown, totally and almost frighteningly distorting her lovely features. Julie was suddenly quite sure that if her hostess had had a rock handy, she must have hurled it at her with all her strength! Turning hastily, she went down the slope in search of the stream.

Once alone with Sir Anthony, Diana said coldly, "It did not take you long to seek out our . . . guest."

There was a frown in his eyes as he said, "I think you know I did not seek her out, Diana."

"Are you suggesting that the shoe was on the other foot, then?"

"I am suggesting that I came to meet you as we had planned and found Mrs. Winslow gazing at the statue. It was a chance meeting and nothing more. A coincidence."

"Really?" Diana's eyes were narrowed. "So many coincidences," she commented coldly. "It was a coincidence that you happened to meet her, and another coincidence that Richard happened upon her in Truro. Would you care to know what *I* think?"

Sir Anthony was silent a moment. Then he said slowly, "Perhaps you would like to hear what I think, Diana. I think that for some unfathomable reason, you are jealous of her."

"Jealous!" She stared at him wide-eyed. "Why on earth would I be jealous of that insignificant little creature? Why, she is practically a dwarf!"

A protest trembled on Sir Anthony's lips—but he had seen Diana in these moods before, and discretion being much the better part of valor at this particular moment, he said merely, "You did give me that impression, my dear, but I did not think it could be true, especially when you have so many more arrows in your quiver than she."

The anger faded from her eyes. "You . . . do not believe that she is . . . well-looking in her way?"

"Is it possible to compare a goddess to a nymph?" he asked softly.

"Oh, dearest Anthony." At last a smile had come to soften Diana's lips and to raise an answering gleam in her eyes. "I fear you grow extravagant."

"You have never protested my so-called extravagance before. And furthermore, it is not extravagance, it is only the truth. There's no one who can compare with you, Diana. However, we are far from the point—"

"The point?" she interrupted, pulling a leaf from a low-hanging branch and tearing it into small pieces. "What point would that be?"

"I beg you'll not be provocative, Diana," he said earnestly, a frown in his eyes. "What do you think of his lordship?"

She let the pieces drift to the ground. "You know my father's plans, Anthony."

He frowned. "I know, too, that you have a very strong will of your own, my dearest Diana, and cannot be coerced unless you are willing to be coerced."

"That is unfair," she said softly. "You know this marriage was none of my designing. My father—"

"Are you so anxious to be a countess?" he interrupted angrily.

Diana pulled another leaf from the branch. "I repeat, you are being unfair. Anthony, dear, the seamstress is at the house—readying my wedding garments. That order was never issued by me. You know the arguments I have had with Father."

"I know that you have told me you have argued with him," he said pointedly.

"It is the truth!" she exclaimed. "But he always refers to the agreement made long ago between himself and Richard's father. They were dear friends. I think he believes that he would be betraying the late Lord Aylsford if he did not hold to their pact. He has never taken my feelings into consideration."

"Then," he said ardently, "if you are not in accord with him, why not run away with me? You know my position. I have money . . ."

"I have told you that I am thinking about it," she said softly.

"You have not told me what you think about the earl," he reminded her.

Diana pressed the leaf against his mouth. "Must we argue about it at this precise moment? We are alone, and now that that little chit has left us, there's no one to disturb us, no one at all, dearest Anthony."

"Oh God, Diana, you witch . . ." Sir Anthony caught her yielding body in his arms and bore her unresisting to the ground.

Following Diana's advice, Julie found the stream. As her hostess had said, it was swift-flowing and there were fish in it, small and silvery, darting swiftly through its depths, while dragonflies, their iridescent wings bearing them above the waters, gleamed brilliantly blue under the sun that sifted through the trees.

There were such streams at home. They fed the lake, a sight now denied to her forever, or, rather, she had denied it to herself by her departure. What would have happened had she remained? She shivered. She would have been a virtual prisoner, chained by the very skills that had secured her freedom! And what did her family think now? Had Lucy communicated with her brother and sister-in-law at the Manor? Did they imagine her dead, and were they making an effort to secure her inheritance? It was quite possible. Another shiver coursed through her as a feeling of loneliness came over her. No one really wanted her.

"Julie!"

She looked up and saw the earl approaching. "Richard." She smiled.

"I saw you by the stream and thought that the mermaid had risen from its depths," he said lightly.

"Are you disappointed to find that it's only me?" she asked.

"On the contrary, I would much rather it were you. I cannot imagine what a mermaid and I would find to discuss."

She had thrilled to the first part of his speech, and it was, she knew, silly to feel singularly let down by the rest of it. The whole of it had been in the realm of teasing. Falling in with his light banter, she said, "I expect a mermaid's main topic would be her dislike for the land and her preference for a sea-girt palace."

"And sunken ships and lost mariners developing scales and tails and relishing their captivity . . . a very pleasant fantasy, Julie, my dear—and do you know, I begin to believe I prefer fantasies to real life."

She glanced up at him and found him staring into some middle distance, his eyes somber. "Do you, Richard? Why?"

"Because . . . one can have his heart's desire, at least for a little while."

"But fantasies do not last," she sighed.

"No." His sigh matched her own. He looked at her. "What have you done to your hair, Julie?"

"My hair?" she asked in surprise.

"Or was it the wind that dressed it, so that it curls about your face? Who was it spoke about sunny locks . . . and many Jasons questing them?"

"Bassanio," Julie said on a breath. *"The Merchant of Venice."*

"Oh, yes, he was speaking of Portia. I wonder if her locks could have been as sunny as yours . . . Bassanio, I seem to remember, also spoke of golden fleece."

"I have never cared for that particular quotation." Julie felt it incumbent upon her to speak lightly and, if possible, to end a conversation that was causing her to feel . . . But she was not sure how she did feel. She added, "It puts me in mind of a sheep. I am sure that is not what Shakespeare intended."

He laughed. "A golden sheep. It does suggest tight little curls. I much prefer flowing locks. Your hair seems longer than when first we met."

"Does it?" she said in some surprise. "I cannot think that it has grown so fast."

"Fast?" he repeated.

"We have not known each other very long, Richard."

"Have we not?" he asked quizzically. "I feel as if we have been friends for aeons." He reached out and took a strand of her hair between his fingers. "It does seem longer. Why did you cut it? Mermaids should never cut their locks." He released the strand of hair.

"Perhaps because when I was sitting on my seabound rock, my golden comb fell into the water and was swept away . . . leaving my locks in a sad tangle."

He laughed and then sobered. "I think—"

"Ah, Richard," Diana called from the slope, "I wondered where you were." She ran lightly down to them. "And Mrs. Winslow."

Her hair was not as neat as it had been earlier, Julie noticed. It hung in elf-locks about her face, and her dress was similarly mussed. And were those grass stains on her skirt?

Inadvertently, another quotation ran through Julie's head: "Let us sit upon the ground and tell sad stories of the death of kings." She doubted that Diana had been engaged in storytelling and mentally chided herself for her suspicions. She said, "I took your advice and found the stream."

"I see you did, and found Richard too." Diana's smile was forced.

"No, I found her," he corrected.

"Oh?"

"The grounds are really lovely here," Julie observed.

"I expect they are," Diana responded unenthusiastically. "I am so used to them. I will be glad to leave and see London." She turned to the earl. "We will live in London, will we not, Richard, dear?"

"I expect we will. However, I have an estate in the country too." He spoke in a rather constricted tone of voice.

Diana rolled her eyes. "Oh dear, I hope you will not tell me that you prefer it to the city? I have spent my entire life here in Cornwall. You must promise London or I shan't marry you!"

"My dear Diana! Is that a threat?" he said lightly.

Diana turned to Julie. "Should it not be, Mrs. Winslow? What do you think?"

"I am not acquainted with London and I am very fond of the country—so perhaps I am not the right person to advise you," Julie replied.

"Oh? Where did you and your husband reside?"

"We traveled about . . . we were not together very long."

"Did he not have an estate?" Diana pursued.

"Yes, but he was not ready to settle down. He was always restless," Julie improvised, hoping that Diana would soon cease her interrogation.

"Ah, I can understand that!" Diana threw a challenging look at the earl. "I do not want to settle down either, not right away, Richard, my love. I hope that we are in accord and that you will take me sailing over the waters to . . . to India and Samarkand."

"Both places are rather far from London, my dear," he commented lightly.

"Yes, but we'll not want to stay in London forever."

"I think," Julie said, "that I had best go in . . . will you excuse me?"

"Of course." Diana caught Richard's hand and swung it back and forth. "Only be careful that you do not get lost."

"I think I can find my way, thank you, Miss Penrose," Julie said. She hurried up a slope, and reaching a tree a short distance from the stairs, she leaned against it to catch her breath. The impression that Diana did not like her had increased. Was it possible that the girl might suspect that she was here under false pretenses? She doubted that. More likely she was the type of female who disliked and distrusted all other members of their sex, seeing them as potential rivals or, possibly, predators like herself.

Julie tensed, wondering why that particular designation had come so quickly to mind. Was she not being overly hard on Diana because she was soon to be the wife of the man she loved with all her heart?

He will never be happy with her.

Julie's tension increased. That statement seemed to have been uttered by someone else, someone other than herself, outside of herself. But that, of course, was ridiculous! Those words were her own, rising unbidden from the depths of her mind. Were they based on that long-ago rock-throwing episode? No, they were predicated on what she had observed in the brief time she had been here. There was a ruthlessness about Diana that was undeniable—at least to those who were not in love with her. Was Richard in love with her? She had believed him intensely attracted to her, but now . . .

A mirthless laugh escaped Julie. The "now" that had come to mind was only a few hours later, and one could not reach any conclusions in so short a time. She did not know Diana, and if she had some queasy feelings about her, these might easily be based on jealousy and resentment—*very* easily, since the girl was soon to become Richard's bride.

Richard.

He had seemed in a most peculiar mood. If they had not been interrupted, possibly she would have been able to find the root of whatever appeared to be troubling him. Was he troubled? He had spoken so oddly, and she had followed his lead in that half-teasing exchange, allowing her hair to be the sole topic of conversation. Yet, of course, that was an oversimplification. They had not really been discussing her hair. In fact, had there been no interruption, they might have abandoned persiflage completely and . . . But she did not want to dwell on what turn their discussion might have taken. Indeed, it was probably just as well that Diana had appeared when she did, to remind them of the reasons why they, or rather he, was there. And what were he and Diana discussing now? Was he whispering sweet nothings in her ear, as the saying went? Tears filled Julie's eyes, and at the same time, her hands knotted into fists, fists she would dearly have loved to shove into Diana's eyes!

The moment that wish rose in her mind, Julie recoiled in horror. It was unlike her to be so vindictive. Yet, in the days that she had been in Richard's company, all manner of new emotions had come to trouble her. They were not only surprising, they were confusing. In the brief time that had passed since she had fled her home, she seemed to have become a different person. More specifically, she felt as though she had awakened from a long, long sleep—an eight-year sleep . . . and would she, after Richard's wedding, drowse again? She hoped so. She did not want to be awake and forever plagued by the knowledge that she would never see him again. Sighing, she directed her steps toward the house. She would spend the hours before dinner in her bed— and hopefully she could sleep.

It was not easy to fall asleep, not with the thoughts that were coursing through her mind, the thoughts and the memories of Richard, which would never, never be dimmed by time! She was certain of that. Still, the need for oblivion was very strong. She undressed with fingers that seemed to be all thumbs and crawled into a bed that received her like a mother's arms, so soft and comfortable it proved to be. It occurred to Julie, as she thankfully felt sleep stealing over her, that she had never experienced mothering arms. If she had children . . . But she never would have children because she could never marry and should not mourn Richard's nuptials—because even were he free, he could not bring her home as his bride.

She awoke to the soft voice of a stranger, and opening her eyes, found a thin, rather pretty woman bending over her bed. She was dressed simply and her apron proclaimed her a servant. She was saying, "Beggin' your pardon, Mrs. Winslow, but it's near time for dinner. I am Ellen and I've come to attend you."

"Oh, have you?" Julie forced a smile, knowing that that hastily arranged dinner was to be given in honor of the engaged couple. She wished that she might plead illness—but Richard knew she was not ill. She must needs dress, must "eat, drink and be merry" over an event that was near to breaking her heart. She said, "I will be glad to avail myself of your services, Ellen. I do not have many garments with me, as you can see." She cast a look at the wardrobe. "But I do have a dinner gown."

"Yes, I have been ironing it, Mrs. Winslow."

"Have you? It needed it . . . And I must wash . . ."

"There is hot water, Mrs. Winslow, in the dressing room."

"Lovely," Julie said, and slipped out of bed.

She was pleased to discover that Ellen had considerable talent when it came to dressing hair. "I hope," she said, "that I did not tear you from Miss Diana's side."

"Oh, no, Mrs. Winslow," the girl answered quickly. "I am called only when there are guests. I used to be Miss Diana's abigail before I was married, but now she has Henriette. She is French."

Julie, staring into her mirror, saw Ellen's slight frown and wondered if she had been put aside to make way for the French maid. She said, "The French are often given more credit for their accomplishments than is their due —merely because so many styles originate in Paris."

"I expect that is true," Ellen said. "There, Mrs. Winslow, is that to your liking?"

Julie, looking into the mirror, was both surprised and pleased to see how well the girl had arranged her hair. It *had* grown a little longer and was at an in-between stage that offered far too many problems for her inexpert fingers. These, however, had been solved with enviable ease by the abigail. Julie was just about to compliment her when she heard a cry, followed by a wild burst of French invective.

Rising swiftly, she opened her door and was in time to see a girl running toward the staircase leading to the upper floor. She was on the stairs when Diana, clad in a lacy peignoir, reached them. Glaring up at her, she said sharply, "You come back here, you little slut. Tomorrow you go back bag and baggage to France—but tonight you are still in my employ and you will finish your task."

"I will not." The girl moved up another step. In strongly accented English, she continued, "I am not a slave, me, to be struck on the face. You do not dismiss me, *mademoiselle*. I, myself, dismiss you. I go—tonight." She ran on up the stairs.

Julie quickly closed her door. She met Ellen's eyes, but made no comment, and nor did the abigail, but she had stiffened and shivered. On witnessing that all-too-telling movement, Julie herself felt cold and guessed what Ellen must have endured when she had served Diana. And this was the woman Richard would marry! He might have some difficulty with the household staff, and that might not be the least of the problems he would encounter in his forthcoming marriage!

Still, her own mother had been impatient with servants, and sometimes unjustly so—but her father had never questioned her running of the household, and furthermore, Richard's eventual domestic problems were none of her concern. Still, given Diana's temper, he might have more than mere domestic problems on his hands. The episode of the rock came to mind, but, again, that had nothing to do with her.

Furthermore, however badly Diana might treat the servants, she would certainly think twice before venting her anger on one she quite obviously admired and must be ready to love—or had she fallen in love at first sight?

If it had been herself, Julie could have answered: Yes. Yet, to imagine Diana in love was difficult. She was so cold, so hard, a diamond to be displayed and admired but . . . Julie sighed and refused to follow that line of reasoning to its logical conclusion. As she had recently discovered, there was nothing logical about love.

And what about Sir Anthony, embittered Sir Anthony, whose eyes had glowed at the sight of Diana? And what about Diana's frowsy hair and the grass stains on her skirt? One could blame the hair on the wind . . . but never the grass stains! That was another line of reasoning that should be abandoned, and quickly! She slowly returned to the dressing table so that Ellen might set a small jet butterfly amidst her curls. It was a delicate and lovely pin and she would treasure it forever —because Richard had insisted on buying it for her.

Two hours later, after a delicious dinner, Julie could hardly believe that the unpleasant scene on the stairs had taken place. Diana, her hair beautifully arranged, was being charm personified. She looked incredibly beautiful in a stylish green gown that seemed to add an extra quotient of color to her brilliant eyes, and she appeared to be in a very good mood, a mood obviously predicated upon Richard's presence. She seemed most attracted to him, and whenever he spoke, she hung on his every word. They were exchanging childhood memories and he appeared extremely interested in her . . . or the memories? One thing was sure, he was entirely oblivious of one "Mrs. Winslow," and beyond a brief greeting, he had been in that condition ever since they had come into the dining room.

Diana had been similarly oblivious to Sir Anthony, who was seated on her right. He had turned his attention to Julie and had done his best to be charming, but it was all too obvious that he was in pain.

Sir Nigel, too, concentrated on his daughter. His complacency was extremely visible and his indulgent attitude obviously fostered his daughter's lack of restraint, her sense that she might do exactly as she pleased and be admired rather than chastised for it.

Probably, Julie decided, Diana had been motherless for quite a long time. She could remember that her own father had exhibited similar signs of that same indulgence after Lady Carleton's death.

Given such a situation, one might be able to understand if not condone Diana's conduct with servants. Yet, the image of the embattled French abigail remained in her mind. The girl would be sent away without references. She would have great difficulty in finding another position, and yet she had dared to be defiant, suggesting that she must have been goaded to the limit. Furthermore, Julie had a feeling that Ellen had had her own problems with Diana.

She glanced at Richard and found her eyes fixed on his hostess. She read admiration in that glance, and wished . . . What did she wish? To tell him about an altercation between mistress and servant? Could she term it a straw in the wind? Possibly it was, but he would not be impressed by such a tale. He had come with some reluctance to assume those obligations arranged by his parents, and he had found the obligation to be beautiful and alluring. What more could a man ask from an arranged marriage?

Julie was glad when it came time for Diana and herself to leave the gentlemen to their brandy. She was not so pleased to find herself alone with Diana in the music room. She could only hope that no heated political discussion would arise to detain Richard and the others. However, Diana did seem disposed to be pleasant, and certainly the surroundings were to her taste.

The chamber was circular and the windows opened onto a small balcony which, in turn, faced the rose arbor. On the ceiling was a beautifully executed painting of Orpheus playing on his lyre while a great crowd of mythological creatures swinging down from trees or emerging from the streams and groves appeared entranced by his music. Pale blue walls were decorated with white bas-reliefs held up by dancing nymphs.

The floor was covered by a pale blue Aubusson carpet and the chairs were covered with either blue or white damask. There was a gilt piano with a painted case, and there was also a harp with a little stool beside it.

Julie looked at the instruments with interest. "Do you play the pianoforte, Miss Penrose?" she asked.

"Please"—Diana smiled at her—"I beg you call me Diana, provided, of course, that you will let me address you as Julie. It is such a lovely name."

"Of course," Julie answered with alacrity. It was very difficult answering to the name of Winslow. Furthermore, it seemed to make the imposture less evident, at least to her mind.

"In answer to your question, Julie, my instrument is the Irish harp. I am part Irish—on my mother's side."

"Oh, are you?"

"Yes, her family traces their ancestry back to Crimm-than, King of Munster, whose relations settled in Wales and Cornwall." Diana's green eyes gleamed. "He was a strong man, and brave! I feel a great kinship with him."

"He must have lived many centuries ago," Julie commented.

"He did. The Romans were still in Britain. He fought against them—very bravely," Diana said proudly. "And what is your heritage, Julie?"

"I do not imagine I can count any Irish kings among my ancestors. There was a Sir Matthew Carleton who fought with Richard III and died with him on Bosworth Field . . . and another ancestor, Sir Charles Carleton, sailed with Drake. Other than that . . . we are a peaceful tribe."

"Oh? Where were you born, Julie?"

"I am from Kent . . . Carleton Manor lies not far from the village of Chilham."

"Kent . . . ah, Romany Marsh . . . they have a smuggling tradition there too."

"Yes, that's true, unfortunately," Julie admitted.

"Unfortunately?" Diana looked surprised. "It is not unfortunate if you like French brandy. There are many here who condone rather than condemn the smugglers."

"I have heard that." Julie nodded.

"What exactly have you heard?" Diana suddenly frowned. She appeared almost angry.

"I have heard that there are smugglers, and wreckers too, in Cornwall."

"There have been, but that is at an end now that Napoleon has been captured—at least, the smuggling is at an end." Diana's eyes gleamed. "I should have loved to be there when the so-called Little Corporal was taken. If I had had the ordering of it, he would have been loaded with chains and his eyes burnt out."

"Oh!" Julie shuddered. "You cannot be serious."

"I am entirely serious!" Diana exclaimed. "My ancestor was known to have treated his prisoners so."

"A thousand years ago," Julie said. "No one in this civilized world would condone so cruel a punishment."

"Perhaps not . . . but the allies were too lenient with him by half! Look at the lives he has wasted. He ought not to be taking his ease on St. Helena, surely!"

"I would not think he was at his ease," Julie said thoughtfully. "He is in exile and will never be able to see France again."

"And your husband is rotting in his grave!" Diana said fiercely. "Does that mean nothing to you?"

Julie, meeting her hostess's fiery eyes, and tardily if horridly reminded of her "late" husband's fate, hastily threw her hands over her face and sank down on an adjacent chair. "Oh," she said with a sob, "it . . . it means everything to me. It means . . . my life."

"Oh, Mrs. Winslow . . . Julie, I am sorry." Diana bent over her. "I did not mean . . ."

"I know you did not," Julie said quickly as she pressed her handkerchief to eyes turned suddenly wet. "I was far too much in love with him, I think." She was glad that Diana could not know that the image which had occasioned these tardy tears was that of Richard. Not for the first time, she wished that she had never met him. To think of him married to this beautiful but blood-thirsty young woman only increased her pain.

Diana followed her apology with another apology, and then, as Julie, acknowledging them, was beginning to believe that the gentlemen would never return to put an end to words that were patently false, they came in, to be greeted most enthusiastically by Diana. Julie, remembering her "bereavement," was less enthusiastic, but since both young men hurried to their hostess's side, her feelings, she realized ruefully, hardly mattered.

"Since we are in the music room, I hope that you will sing for us, Diana," Sir Anthony said warmly.

Diana gave him a teasing glance. "I might," she said, "but perhaps Julie would sing or . . . perhaps play for us?"

"Oh, no." Julie achieved a realistic sigh. "I am in mourning."

"My poor child," Sir Nigel said sympathetically, "you are very young to have sustained so tragic a loss."

Julie flushed as she said quickly, "There are many women much younger than I who have suffered similar losses. But please, let us not dwell on such matters. I myself am eager to hear Diana play."

"As am I," the earl said. "Will it be the piano or the harp?"

"It must be the harp," Sir Anthony said, and then added quickly, "if . . . if that is what you wish, Diana."

Sir Nigel had been frowning, but he said, "I agree with Anthony. My daughter's a most accomplished harpist. And though I may be prejudiced, I will say that she is a fine singer too. Perhaps Richard has a favorite song or ballad he would like to hear.''

" 'Barbara Allen' has always pleased me," Richard said.

"That is one of my favorites too." Sir Anthony smiled at Diana.

"Very well, poor Barbara it will be." Diana sat down and ran her fingers over the harp strings, and in a moment she began to sing the ballad.

As the music progressed, Julie stifled a little gasp of surprise. Diana was an excellent musician. Her voice, slightly husky, was both lovely and beguiling. She also sang most expressively, suggesting that she had a strong sense of the dramatic. She delineated Barbara Allen's anger at the toast that had slighted her most effectively. She was also coldly oblivious of her dying lover's pleas. In all, the performance was compelling, and her small audience was properly fascinated.

Richard, Julie noted, could not take his eyes off the singer. He stood as one entranced, which, undoubtedly, he was. A feeling not unlike a physical pain filled Julie, and the small room suddenly appeared even smaller. Since she was sitting in shadow and close to the hall door, which Sir Nigel had left open, Julie rose and quietly glided out. As she came into the hall, she saw that a side door had been open to let in the evening breeze, and she gratefully came out to take deep breaths and fan herself with one hand.

"Are you not well, then, Julie?"

Julie started, and turning, found the earl behind her. "Oh, you should not have left the music room, Richard!" she protested. "What will Diana think?"

"Must I repeat my question?" he asked worriedly. "You do look pale, Julie."

"I cannot think why. I am only warm. It was very

close in the music room. I noticed it when we first came there. And I do think that we must go back, do not you?''

"We will go back only if you are feeling more the thing, Julie," he said stubbornly.

"Oh, Richard." She put a protesting hand on his arm. "What will Diana think? She will be hurt and angry at her fiancé leaving in the midst of her song—and she will be well within her rights."

"She has an audience," he said stubbornly. "She is singing 'The Rising in the North' and it is tolerably long. We've missed only a verse or two. But if you are sure that you are recovered, we will go."

She gazed up at him, thinking unhappily that she would never, never recover from the malady afflicting her, but she said lightly, "I am much refreshed, Richard, dear. Do let us hurry!"

Diana was not singing the ballad Richard had mentioned when they returned. She had changed to "Men of Harlech." She sang it well, with flashing eyes and martial tone. Julie, however, had an uncomfortable feeling that the rousing ballad reflected the singer's anger at her fiancé's seeming defection. However, once Diana had struck the last chord, Richard clapped loudly.

"That was splendid, my dear!" he cried.

Diana gave him a challenging stare. "I fear you did not hear enough of it to justify such a compliment, Richard."

"Come, my dear Diana," Sir Nigel said soothingly, "Richard was absent no more than a minute or two." He turned to Julie. "I hope you are not ill, Mrs. Winslow."

"I was only a little warm," Julie explained.

"It is close in here," he agreed. "Let us all take a stroll in the gardens. I will have the servants bring some lights."

"There is also a very bright moon tonight," Sir Anthony said.

Julie, remembering her widowhood, gladly made the most of it. "If you will excuse me," she breathed. "The moon . . ." She shook her head. "When Christopher and I were in Brussels before the . . . But I must not burden you with my . . . memories. I will, if you are kind enough to excuse me, go to bed."

Amidst a chorus of sympathy—one, she noticed, in which Richard did not join—Julie, receiving that permission, thankfully retired to her chamber. The moon, never brighter, seemed to reach every corner, gilding the room with silver—and providing her with memories of herself and Richard on board his yacht.

Ellen, hurrying to help her disrobe, found Julie weeping. There was no doubting the realism of her sobs, and the abigail, never doubting the cause of her grief, did her best to comfort her on the death of her husband.

8

Julie had planned to plead a sick headache and thus remain aloof from the earl and his fiancée. However, the morning sun, the warbling birds, and the scents of the garden coming through her windows combined to abolish the melancholy of the previous evening. And when Ellen brought her the news that her hostess begged that Julie join herself and the gentlemen on a ride to Looe Pool, she assented readily. Then, belatedly, remembering that she had no riding habit, she sent word of that lack via Ellen, who returned with one of Diana's habits. It was, of course, too large for her, but the abigail caught up the hem and made a few alterations in the waist, with the result that she was ready even before her hostess.

Now, riding beside Sir Anthony, her eyes on the earl and his fiancée, who were several paces ahead of them, Julie was regretting her impulsive acquiescence. Richard's greeting had been cool that morning, and as they had ridden out of the stableyard he had attached himself to Diana and there he had remained without so much as a backward glance at her.

Sir Anthony also seemed withdrawn, and it was not hard to guess that he was suffering over Diana's rejection. She had hardly spoken to him. Her attention had been riveted on the earl. Indeed, Julie thought resentfully, they acted as if no one but themselves existed! Neither of them had had so much as a backward look for those riding behind them, which, of course, she realized belatedly, was just as it ought to be, since they were so soon to be married. She guessed that a deeper understanding had taken place on the previous evening. Probably Sir Anthony, all too aware that he was *de trop,* had gone home and the engaged pair had been left alone in that all-prevasive moonlight.

"The pool is misnamed, you know," Sir Anthony observed, breaking the silence that had ensued between them for the last quarter of an hour.

She was still not in the mood for conversation, but she was also unwilling to entertain the thoughts currently racing through her mind. She said, "I understand that it is a lake."

"It is a large lake," he emphasized, "and while we would like to believe that the Lady dwelt there and reached up to catch King Arthur's sword, well, it would not be a particularly habitable spot for a female whose favorite wearing apparel was a white silk material called samite."

"Shame on you," Julie laughed. "I fear you are an iconoclast, sir."

"Is Arthur one of your idols?"

"No, there's another knight I prefer."

"Sir Lancelot, of course?"

She shook her head. "No, I am far more partial to Sir Gareth, the so-called Kitchen Knight," Julie said thoughtfully.

"You are very practical." He grinned. "If you were ever to experience a shortage of servants, you could recruit him."

"Actually, I was thinking more of his love for the damsel Lynette. I prefer her to Guinevere."

"Ah, and what is your opinion of Iseult of the White Hands?"

"I wonder if anyone had white hands in those days."

He laughed. "My dear Mrs. Winslow, I fear you do not have a romantic nature. You should, you know."

"Why?"

"Can you not guess?" He leaned toward her.

She shook her head. "I admit myself at a loss, Sir Anthony."

"Well, had you lived in the days of the minstrels, you must have figured in more than one lay. All the beautiful women did."

"Sir Anthony"—Julie looked at him in surprise—"I fear you grow far too extravagant."

"No," he said thoughtfully, "and I wonder why you consider it necessary to dissemble."

"To . . . dissemble, sir?"

"Surely you must be well aware of the image your mirror reveals."

Julie flushed and looked away from him, discovering as she did that the earl and Diana were no longer in view. "I think we have fallen too far behind, Sir Anthony," she said.

"Why should you think that?" he asked edgily. "I am quite sure our friends do not bemoan our absence."

She looked at him and found his eyes somber. Undoubtedly, for all his semiflirting with herself, he was miserable over Diana's defection. In spite of the fact that her parents and Richard's had arranged the betrothal, Sir Anthony must have been hoping against hope that the earl would not abide by that parental decision. Her heart went out to her unhappy companion —especially since she could match him woe for woe. She said, "I do not imagine that Diana would have insisted that you come on this excursion had she been indifferent, Sir Anthony."

"Do you not?" His laugh held cadences of bitterness. "You do not know her. Sometimes I think she delights in causing pain."

Julie, remembering the scene with the French maid,

was inclined to agree with him—but agreement was not what he craved, she was sure. She said, "Oh, no, I am sure you are wrong."

"You would not understand that, would you?" he said. "You are so considerate, so gentle . . . a man would always know were he stood with you."

"I think . . ." Julie began, and paused as Diana suddenly cantered up to them. She rode well and she looked magnificent on horseback; Julie had noticed that earlier. Her habit, made of pelisse cloth, was as green as her eyes, and though she was wearing a matching hat, a few strands of her dark hair had become loosened and curled most becomingly about her face. However, her beauty was marred by her obvious annoyance—or would "anger" be the better term?

"You have fallen rather far behind," she observed coldly. "We were wondering what had happened to you."

The abruptness of her tone must have startled her horse, for it began to snort and dance about restlessly. As Anthony reached out to catch the bridle, Diana brought her crop down hard on the horse's rump, causing the animal to whinny and rear.

"Oh!" Julie exclaimed indignantly. "That was hardly necessary, Diana!"

"You are quite right," Sir Anthony agreed. "One does not take one's pique out on a helpless animal."

Diana glared at him. "You are presuming to give me lessons in riding, Anthony?"

"And in deportment," he responded sharply.

Diana, visiting a furious look on him, set spurs to her horse and cantered away with Sir Anthony in pursuit. He caught up with her a short distance down the road, and reaching for her bridle, brought her to a stop that almost unseated her.

"What are you about?" she cried shrilly.

"That is a question I wish to ask you, Diana," he returned coldly. " What is the matter with you? I have never seen you in so contrary a mood."

She said coldly, "Why should my moods trouble you, Anthony?"

"You know why," he responded in a lower voice.

"Do I?"

"Only last week you were telling me that you could not abide Richard, and now—"

"And now I find him much changed," she said. "Indeed, I would not have known him."

"This is not surprising, since you were only seven when you parted."

"One can form lasting opinions, even at seven."

"But the opinion is obviously not lasting . . . in fact, you are attracted to him. Is that not so?" he questioned pointedly.

"If I am, it is just as well, since my father is determined that we marry."

"He would not be so determined if you showed any reluctance," he said bitterly. "You've been fast and loose with me all these years, Diana!"

"All these years—numbering three."

"You know I have cared for you longer than that. Had I not been on the Peninsula—"

"You knew I was promised to Richard. Furthermore, I do not see why you are complaining. You seem perfectly happy with the widow. I had not thought she would appeal to you."

He stared at her in surprise. "I begin to believe that you are jealous," he said slowly.

"I . . . jealous of *her*? I assure you that I am not—even though I am quite aware that you have been doing your utmost to make me jealous. It is not a successful ploy, dear Anthony."

"A ploy?" He raised his eyebrows. "I assure you I

had no intention of making you jealous, Diana. Why should I? You have been doing your utmost to show me how unimportant I am to you."

There was a pause before Diana said, "You are not unimportant to me, Anthony. I have told you that I had no choice. My father's heart is set on this marriage."

He moved his horse closer to hers. "I once told you how you might circumvent your father's wishes. You refused. You were his only child and he was your only father."

"You are pleased to be sarcastic." She glared at him.

"I am not being sarcastic. I am telling you no more than the truth, and you know it. Well, you have pleased your father. You are to be married to Lord Aylsford, and why should it trouble you that I enjoy the company of Mrs. Winslow?"

"Oh, so you do enjoy her company?" she questioned sharply. "I do not find that very flattering."

"Flattering?"

"After all your words of love and undying devotion to me . . . and now you seem to be *enjoying* the company of that spineless little nonentity."

"She is most certainly not a nonentity. Furthermore, I find great sweetness to her. She is as good as she is beautiful, Diana."

"Beautiful?" Diana's eyes widened. "You find her beautiful? Surely you jest!"

"She is beautiful, not in the way that you are beautiful, Diana. She is your opposite in nearly every respect."

Diana had stiffened during his defense of Julie, and for a moment it seemed to him as if she could not find words enough to achieve an answer. Finally she said icily, "If she were not my . . . opposite in nearly every way, dear Anthony, I should be most unhappy—since she reminds me of a little white mouse!"

He laughed. "She reminds me of a nymph. She is really most beguiling."

"She is also a widow," Diana snapped. "Her heart is broken. Have you forgotten that?"

"Broken hearts can be mended, Diana."

"And you are going to furnish the glue, Anthony?"

He said thoughtfully, "Someone must, when . . ." But Diana did not wait to hear the rest of his reply. Head held high, she spurred her horse forward. After a split second, Anthony rode after her.

At the same moment that Diana had left Julie's side, pursued by Sir Anthony, the earl had joined Julie. "What happened?" he asked.

She shook her head. "I am not quite sure. Diana . . ." She was about to tell him about her mistreatment of the horse, but caught herself in time. It hardly behooved her to criticize her hostess and his fiancée. She said merely, "She appeared to have some difficulty in controlling her mount."

"Yes, he's a restive creature. Diana has always preferred a spirited horse—even as a child, she insisted on a fractious pony."

Julie longed to tell him that his bride-to-be appeared to consider riding a contest between mistress and steed in which she must needs always emerge the winner. Furthermore, she had a strong suspicion that Diana's love of mastery extended far beyond horses. She thought of Sir Anthony. Diana was kind to him one moment and indifferent the next. He never knew where he stood with her, and it appeared that she always had the upper hand.

Julie had a feeling that the girl would use the same tactics with Richard, and she wished she might give him the benefit of her observations. Unfortunately, these would not be welcome, even were she to commit such a solecism. He was obviously attracted to her and probably delighted that she had turned out so well.

"What is the matter, Julie?"

She started. She had been so deep in thought that she had almost forgotten that he was beside her. Her quick movement had caused her horse to snort and dance. "Steady, steady, there," she murmured, thinking that her command must needs extend to herself. She smiled up at the earl. "There is nothing the matter, Richard. Why should you imagine that there was?"

He brought his mount closer. "You seemed abstracted. And why did you not try to catch up with us, you and your . . . escort?"

She gave him a startled glance. His tone had been edged with anger. "Can you not guess, Richard?" she asked in no little surprise.

"Are you presenting me with a conundrum?" His frown was even more in evidence. "I am not skilled at solving puzzles."

"This solution is simple enough. We thought that you would want to be alone with your fiancée."

The frown remained. "That was very thoughtful indeed, my dear Julie, but since we had agreed to ride *together,* the four of us, such consideration was rather misplaced." He urged his horse even closer, and reaching out, caught her arm. "Do you not realize that . . ." he began, but came to a stop as Diana, with Sir Anthony behind her, came riding back.

"Ah, here you are!" Diana exclaimed. "I thought you would have gone to the lake, Richard." She was smiling, but her gaze, straying in Julie's direction, was chill.

"There seems to be confusion all around," Sir Anthony commented lightly. " Still, now that we are all together, let us continue on to the pool."

"An excellent idea, Anthony," Diana said. "And I suggest that in order to avoid further confusion, we go

two by two like the animals in the ark." Riding on
ahead, she signaled to Richard. "We will lead the
procession, my dear. Come."

It seemed to Julie that Richard's smile was forced.
Certainly his tone of voice was cool as he responded.
"That is an excellent idea, my dear." He rode slowly up
to join her.

The rest of the ride was without incident. Sir
Anthony, once more beside Julie, seemed in a better
humor. He took pains to point out various landmarks
on the way to Looe Pool and also regaled her with some
of the local legends. She managed to listen most of the
time. However, warring against her total attention was
her interrupted conversation with Richard. What had he
wanted to tell her before Diana returned? He had
seemed annoyed that she and Sir Anthony had fallen
behind. Did he suspect . . . ?

"At last, here we are," Richard called back. "The
deep domain of Arthur, King of Britain."

"The once and future king!" Julie corroborated.

Sir Anthony cocked an eye at her. "Will you be
telling me that you are among those who believe that
Arthur and his knights lie sleeping in some underground
cavern awaiting the signal to rise and save us in our
greatest hour of peril?"

"It is a pleasant superstition, do you not agree?"

"I am glad you called it a superstition," he laughed.
"There are some, and Sir Nigel's grandfather among
them, who credited and still might credit the tale."

"Gracious," Julie giggled. "It would take him some
time to get the stiffness out of his limbs after a
thousand-year sleep."

Another crack of laughter escaped Sir Anthony. "I
had never thought of that, but yes, he and his knights
might need considerable limbering up before they were
ready to ride into battle."

"You seem pleasantly merry." Diana joined them.

Her gaze, as before, avoided Julie and lingered on Sir Anthony's face. "Might we share the joke?"

Sir Anthony's smile vanished. "It is nothing that would bear repetition." He turned back to Julie. "Come, let me show you the fatal spot where the sword was supposedly thrown . . . the water there is very blue—the color of your eyes, my dear Mrs. Winslow."

"Fie on you, good Sir Anthony." Diana's laugh was brittle. She turned to Julie. "He has compared those waters to my eyes, which, as you can see, are green."

She received a cool stare from Sir Anthony as he said meaningfully, "The lake is changeable, Diana, as changeable as a woman's will."

"Sometimes a woman's will is changed for her, dear Anthony." Diana had spoken in a low voice. Evidently, Julie reasoned, she did not want to be overheard by the earl, who was only a short distance away. However, Diana did not seem to mind that Julie heard her. Julie guessed that the girl was once more trying to lure Anthony to her side. It must please her to hold him in thrall . . . and would she wax, by turns, warm and cold, until Richard placed his ring on her finger? Julie's dislike for Diana increased, and concurrent with that was her concern for Richard's future happiness.

He wanted to settle down. His preference was not for London, but Diana had a strong will. Their life together would not be easy, and Julie had a sudden conviction that the happiness that he so obviously desired must elude him. Indeed, it was more than possible that three people—herself, Sir Anthony, and Richard—would be unhappy. And what of Diana? Julie felt cold. She might be very happy—because judging from her actions, she might very well thrive on the misery of others.

Could that be true?

Julie stared into the pellucid waters of the lake and saw their images caught there as if in a crystal ball, or, as it was said in the Bible, a glass, darkly. They were three people bound by the will of a fourth, a dark-haired, green-eyed mermaid. Mermaids were known to drag sailors down to their coral palaces and keep them there until they died. Only the mermaid survived, because she could not love and had no soul. Julie shivered again.

"Are you cold, Mrs. Winslow?" Sir Anthony asked solicitously.

"A little," she lied, suddenly wanting to be away from there. "I think I had best ride back."

"You cannot go alone," Sir Anthony said quickly. "I will accompany you."

"We will all ride back," Diana said decisively. She turned her cool gaze on Julie. "I hope, Mrs. Winslow, that you are not coming down with a chill."

Meeting Diana's eyes, she found them devoid of sympathy. She was tempted to tell her that she was only tired, but a second thought caused her to say, "I do feel a bit queasy. In fact, judging from the signs, I think it would be better if I went to bed as soon as I returned."

"Oh dear, I am sorry. I have some excellent physic," Diana said. "I will see that you have it as soon as we are back at the Hall."

"You are kind." Julie managed a smile. "But I have learned that rest will restore me quickly enough."

"And"—the earl came forward—"had you better ride? Let me take you up before me."

She had a strong desire to avail herself of that offer, but a glance at Diana quelled it. The beauty's mouth was turned down and her green eyes were blazing. The mermaid was waxing wroth, as an old ballad might put it. Julie said, "No, thank you, Richard, I am able to ride that short distance." Suiting her action to her words, she went immediately to her horse—but Sir Anthony was there before her, helping her to mount. A

side glance at Diana revealed that this kindly gesture
had brought an even brighter blaze to her eyes. Julie,
feeling rather uncomfortable, clicked to her horse and
cantered back along the way they had come.

The moon, a day past its full glory, was shining
through the windows. Julie had never liked to have the
curtains closed, not even as a child, and contrary to the
beliefs of many, she found no peril in the evening air.
Consequently, once Ellen had undressed her and left the
room, Julie pulled back the curtains and threw open the
windows. The sound of crickets reached her, and the
moonlight was beguiling. Despite the presence of that
silvery orb, it was not quite dark and it would be very
pleasant to stroll through the gardens at this hour.

Julie had stayed in her chamber ever since she had
returned from the lake. Now, after a long nap, she felt
restless and confined. Another day was nearly over, and
the inevitable was closer. Soon, she thought
despondently, she would be able to measure the time in
hours rather than days, and the walls of her room
seemed to be moving closer as in those dread dungeons
where tyrants of old shut the enemies they wanted to
torture before destroying.

She shuddered at the analogy. Love made one happy.
Thwarted love caused one to grow morbid. She was, she
realized miserably, learning a great deal about an
emotion most women experienced earlier. At this
moment she wished that she had never experienced it at
all—but she had and still did, and it rendered her
restless. Indeed, at this moment she was finding it
impossible to remain here in this borrowed chamber in a
house where preparations were being made for a
wedding that would bring all the county to the church
and, later, to the great hall downstairs, where the bride
would be toasted. Ellen had described her gown, a pure
silk made for her in Paris. Her veil had belonged to her

grandmother and was fashioned from fine lace and would extend over half the length of the aisle. She and Richard would make a handsome couple.

"Oh God, God, God," Julie groaned. "I cannot bear to think of it."

Going to the armoire, she dressed as hastily as she could and hurried down the stairs. The house was quiet. Probably Sir Anthony and Richard were in the music room listening to one of Diana's stirring ballads. Julie cocked an ear for the sounds of a harp, but heard nothing—but she would hear nothing if the door was closed. In another moment she had found the side door and was outside in the fragrant air.

The mingled scents of the flowers and the drowsy sounds of birds settling down for the night, coupled with the too-whoos of the waking owls and the chorus of crickets and frogs, reminded Julie of her many walks with her father—taken, as now, in the cool of the evening.

They had discussed the coming journey to Brighton . . . A wave of anguish rolled over her. The hectic turn her life had taken had left her very little time to mourn. Even her last days at home, she had been prevented from dwelling overmuch on his death, and now, the fact that he was gone and that there was no one to whom she might turn for solace or advice seemed particularly depressing. Never had she felt so utterly alone, not even in the days following her divorce, when she had lived in a veritable vacuum—ignored by parents and siblings alike. If she might have had her father with her, she could have borne this new sorrow more easily. However, had he survived, there would have been no sorrow. She would not have been forced to flee from her home in the middle of the night aided by her nephew. She and her father would have been in Brighton and the earl unknowing of her existence.

"Mrs. Winslow! You are better, then?"

Startled, Julie looked up to find Sir Anthony coming toward her. "Y-yes," she stammered, wishing that he had not come upon her unawares. "I am feeling much more myself, thank you. I expect it was the rest that restored me."

"I am glad to hear it." He came to stand beside her. "We missed you at dinner. Indeed, it was deadly dull without your presence."

"Gracious, Sir Anthony, I fear you grow extravagant," she chided.

"No," he said seriously. "You have no idea what a palliative you have been—"

"A palliative, sir?" she repeated. "I think I must still accuse you of extravagance."

"You may not, Mrs. Winslow. I am speaking the truth." He moved a little closer to her, saying earnestly, "I am sure that you must have guessed that we, Diana and I, have known each other a long time—most of our lives, indeed. Our parents were good friends and we were much together. I once imagined myself in love with her, and she . . . she was not discouraging. Indeed, she gave me to understand . . . But no matter, I do not wish to dwell on the past, Mrs. Winslow. I . . . I know that your husband met a cruel death and that you are in mourning, but grief cannot last forever—"

"Sir, I was much in love with my husband," Julie interrupted. His confidences, together with his closeness, was making her nervous. Furthermore, she did not quite know how to deal with him. Her experience with men had been so swiftly curtailed, and yet she felt that Sir Anthony had more on his mind than his late disappointment over Diana. He was standing even closer to her and he was breathing as though he had just run a race.

"I know you were in love with your husband," he said. "I have been much in love myself—that is why I can tell you that it is an emotion that can pass with amazing swiftness. You miss your husband sorely now, but later there will be a void, an emptiness that will need to be filled. You might not agree with me at this moment, but later you will understand. Please, let me have your direction before you go. I . . . we must not lose sight of each other. Oh, Mrs. Winslow . . . Julie, please . . ." He suddenly caught her in his arms.

She struggled against him in vain. She could not free herself from that viselike embrace. His mouth covered hers—his kiss was passionate and invading. It seemed to last forever!

"Oh," she cried when he finally released her. "How . . . how could you, when you know . . ." She burst into tears.

"Mrs. Winslow . . . Julie, dearest Julie," he said huskily, catching her in his arms again. "I beg you will—"

"Let me go!" she sobbed.

"But, my love, my dearest, you must listen," he began.

"I think, Anthony, that Julie does not return your passion," remarked a cool voice.

He moved back hastily, his arms falling to his sides. "Diana!" he exclaimed in accents of strong chagrin.

Released from his grasp, Julie fled, not stopping until she had reached the door. She came in swiftly and had gained the stairs when she was confronted by the earl.

"Julie!" He looked at her concernedly. "What is the matter, my dear?"

She stared at him, vainly trying to blink back her tears. "Nothing," she said on a sob she could not control.

"Nothing?" he repeated. "I do not believe you. What has upset you, my dear? Tell me."

"Nothing, it was nothing at all," she assured him, striving to get command of herself. "I must go to my room."

"Not yet." He caught her arm. "Tell me, my dearest." He brushed a fallen lock back from her face. "Please tell me: what is the matter?"

"The matter?" she repeated half-hysterically as she tried to get away. "Oh, Richard, please, please, let me go," she moaned. "I should not have left my room. Oh God, I should not be here under false pretenses. It is an affront to . . . to everyone."

"Hush," he said almost fiercely. "If you were not here . . ." He paused. "You could not have gone back by yourself, my darling. I would not have had a moment's peace—knowing you were alone, innocently inviting the attentions of strangers. You *are* an innocent, you know."

"I have told you—" she began.

"Do not mention your so-called disgrace again," he ordered. "Indeed, were it possible . . ." He broke off with a frown. "But no matter, you cannot think of traveling alone, ever. Indeed, I am more than half . . ." Again he broke off as Diana came in.

"Oh, here you are, Julie," she said coolly. "I hope that you will find it in your heart to forgive Anthony. He is most contrite."

"Why?" the earl demanded curtly. "Why is he most contrite?"

"It is nothing, Richard," Julie said hastily. "He seemed to . . . to come out of nowhere when I was walking in the gardens. He startled me."

He looked down at her half-quizzically, half-sternly. "Is that all?"

"That is all," Diana corroborated. She smiled at the earl. "The gardens are very pleasant in the moonlight—will you come walking with me, Richard, my dearest?"

There was a slight hesitation before he said, "Of course, Diana." He bent a stern look on Julie. "You had best go to bed, Julie."

"I will," she said. "I came down only for a breath of air. Good night, Diana."

"Good night, Julie. I will hope that you are more yourself in the morning."

"I am certain I shall be," Julie assured her. She hurried up the stairs. On reaching her chamber, she flung herself on the bed. Her emotions were in a turmoil. Diana had seen her with Sir Anthony and then with Richard. What could she think?

She had seemed calm enough. It was, of course, possible that she was so confident of her power to charm that she thought nothing of finding Julie clutched in Sir Anthony's arms. Fortunately, there had been nothing compromising in Richard's attitude, at least when Diana had come upon them. Yet, she had seemed concerned, and that concern had, unfortunately, increased when Diana mentioned Sir Anthony. Would she suspect an attachment? No, how could she, when none existed?

"None?" Julie whispered, remembering that he had called her "my darling." Had he? Or had she dreamed it? No, he had and . . . But she must not build castles on such a sandy foundation.

Richard, as he had proved more than once, was by nature chivalrous and honorable. Even were he to feel a partiality for her, he would not heed it. Diana was his promised bride and in a matter of a few days she would be his wife . . . walking proudly down the aisle in her silken white gown from Paris and the lacy veil that would cover half the aisle! That was inevitable, just as it was inevitable that she, Julie Carleton, would miss him all the days of her life.

9

The clock chimed the hour of five, and then six. Julie, lying in bed, had tried vainly to summon the elusive Morpheus again, but that stubborn deity remained absent, and finally, at seven, she wearily arose and performed her ablutions. Generally, the application of a sponge dipped in cold water and applied over her face and body restored her. She did not feel in the least restored this morning, and a glance in the mirror revealed that her lack of sleep had left circles under her eyes. There was also a heaviness in her breast which she would have preferred to attribute to the same cause, but were she to be entirely truthful with herself, she could not.

The arrival of another day—a day that meant seeing Richard all too often and, perhaps, fending off Sir Anthony, as well as dealing with Diana's possible anger if either young man seemed to be paying too much attention to her. It was a damnable situation and would not grow any better. It was futile to wish that she were a thousand miles away. She could have been three-hundred-odd miles away if she had been able to remain at home or . . . But it was equally futile to dwell on possibilities. She was here, and here she must needs remain until that ceremony that would bind the man she loved to a woman she was well on the way of loathing.

"My gracious, Mrs. Winslow!" Ellen exclaimed

when she came to dress Julie. "You look that pale. Do you think you are well enough to be up? Perhaps it would be better if you was to stay in bed this day."

Julie was tempted to abide by her suggestion—but a restlessness had invaded her. She needed to be up and out, or possibly she would explore the library if Sir Nigel were not occupying it. She had not visited it yet, but she had glimpsed it in passing, and the floor-to-ceiling shelves of books had looked most inviting. Furthermore, she doubted that either Richard or Diana would intrude on that particular sanctuary.

She had tea and toast in her room, and it was close on ten when she finally came down. Much to her relief, there was no one about when she descended the stairs. She went down the hall, and opening the door to the library, saw that there was no one at the huge Chippendale desk. She came in quickly and was about to go to the shelves when Sir Nigel said, "Ah, Mrs. Winslow, good morning."

Julie started, and turning, saw him rising from a wing chair that had been facing the fireplace. "Oh, I had not meant to disturb you, sir," she said quickly.

"But you have not, my dear," he responded cordially. "Am I to infer that you are a reader?"

"Yes, sir," she said shyly. "I have always enjoyed reading."

"Have you?" His eyes lighted as he added approvingly, "You are to be commended. I have tried to encourage my daughter to do more reading, but she, I fear, prefers horseback riding, walking, and swimming to such sedentary pursuits. I expect that she will find these much curtailed when she marries."

"Lord Aylsford has a country estate," Julie said.

"I do not imagine they will be spending a great deal of time in the country. My daughter has long protested our provincial ways," Sir Nigel said ruefully.

"Has she? I think it is beautiful here."

"Yes, it is, and I am glad that you agree with me. I should very much like to take you around the estate this morning, but unfortunately, I have an appointment with one of my tenants. Meanwhile—"

"Ah, here you are, Mrs. Winslow. I have been looking for you. I have been, I think, extremely remiss in my duties as hostess."

Julie turned hastily, as did Sir Nigel, to find Diana standing in the doorway. "Ah, good morning, my dear." Her father smiled.

"Good morning, father." Diana, dressed, as always, for riding, smiled at Julie. "I do hope you are feeling better this morning, Mrs. Winslow . . . Julie, I mean."

"Yes, I am, thank you," Julie responded.

"I am glad. I had hoped to show you some of the estate."

"Ah," Sir Nigel said, "I was just telling Mrs. Winslow that I had wanted to take her about, but as you know, old Jack Borlase is ailing and his wife has begged that I visit them."

"Yes, I know," Diana said. "Poor old man." She looked at Julie. "He was a miner, and one can work too long at that trade. But be that as it may, since you will probably not come this way again soon, let me take you over our property."

"You must go," Sir Nigel urged. "My daughter is a much better guide than I, and well up on the local legends."

"If Julie is interested in legends," Diana said.

"Oh, I am," Julie assented. The thought of being in Diana's company did not particularly appeal to her— but still, it would keep her from meeting Richard, and that, she reminded herself, was what she wanted. She said, "I would be delighted to come with you, Diana."

"Good," she exclaimed. "But you must change into my habit—we will need to ride."

"I will do so immediately," Julie said.

An hour later, mounted on Arthur, the horse she had ridden the previous day, Julie followed Diana out of the stableyard. It was a fine day for riding. There was a brisk breeze and it was not too warm. In fact, there were a few clouds in the sky that might presage an afternoon rain—but by that time they would be safely back in the house. She had needed to reassure Ellen on that point. The abigail had, in fact, begged her not to go.

"You wasn't feeling your best yesterday, Mrs. Winslow," she had protested when called to help Julie into the habit. Speaking with what Julie guessed was unusual frankness, Ellen had said insistently, "You mustn't ride too far. Miss Diana's tireless in the saddle, and since you are not at your best . . ."

"I will insist that I must return immediately I begin to feel weary," Julie had promised, thinking that the abigail looked almost frightened.

"You do that, Mrs. Winslow," Ellen had urged. "This estate covers a good deal of ground, and not all of it is safe—unless you are an experienced rider like Miss Diana."

"I, too, am experienced," Julie had assured her. "I come from Kent, and our estate is also large."

She was pondering Ellen's admonitions as she and Diana, riding side by side, traversed a long stretch of uncultivated ground. It was slow going, and Diana, almost echoing the abigail, said, "I hope you are not growing too tired, Julie. Given your illness yesterday, perhaps I should not have asked you. It is just that I did not have a fitting today. The rest of the week will be very busy for me."

Julie, wincing at the implications of that remark, was glad that her anguish did not color her speech as she replied, "No, I am feeling quite myself again, thank you."

"You do look well. One would never know that you were not at your best."

"You are kind to tell me so." Julie forced a smile.

"I am not being kind. I am being honest, Julie," Diana assured her. "In fact, I will tell Richard that he has been refining far too much on your illness. He was wont to borrow trouble even when he was little. I expect he has told you that we have known each other a long time."

"Yes," Julie said. "Since you were children."

"Can you imagine that we were betrothed even then? We both rebelled against the idea. Indeed, I was half-afraid to see him again. I had convinced myself that I loved Sir Anthony and I had decided that I would hate Richard. Fortunately, seeing him again changed all that for us both. He has told me that he never would have believed that the ugly little girl I once was would grow up into the woman I have become. Indeed, he said something very silly. I was inclined not to believe him, but he assures me that it is the truth."

"Oh? What did he say?"

"Well . . ." Diana hesitated. "I scarcely like to repeat it. It will sound so conceited on my lips."

"Do tell me," Julie urged.

"He said . . ." Diana laughed self-consciously. "He said that I was a legend come alive."

"He could hardly say anything different. You are very beautiful, and I, for one, cannot believe that you were ever ugly."

"You are uncommonly kind, Julie." Diana appeared surprised. "It is not often that women are kind to each other. At least, that has been my experience, and I should imagine that you, too, must have suffered similarly."

"No." Julie shook her head, wondering what Diana would say were she aware that Julie knew no women and, in fact, had no friends at all save Richard, so soon to be lost . . . no, not soon, *already* lost, if he were as contented with his bride as Diana had implied. Last night he had not seemed . . . But she would not think about that.

"You are fortunate in your women friends, then, Julie," Diana pursued. Before Julie could answer, she continued, "And with your gentlemen friends as well, I think."

"On occasion," Julie replied, thinking of Richard again, and of her nephew, who could also be counted as a friend. She did not include Sir Anthony, and preferred not to remember last night's episode. Indeed, she did not want to dwell on either man—even though she was miserably sure that Richard would not be forgotten were she to live another fifty years—a prospect that made her only more melancholy.

"We will turn off here," Diana said suddenly. She pointed to a narrow path. "This will take us to our very own Logan stones."

Julie looked up, startled to find that while she had been deep in thought, her horse had borne her farther down the lonely path Diana had chosen. And now the sound of the sea was in her ears and its salty smell in her nostrils. "What are the Logan stones?" she asked.

Diana pulled her horse to a stop, and as Julie followed her example, she said, "A Logan stone, or, as you might put it, a rocking stone is actually a pair of rocks balanced one on top of the other. There are many of them here in Cornwall and also in Devonshire on the moors."

"Oh, yes, I think Richard did tell me that there is such a formation on your property—the Kissing Rocks."

"Quite. Did he tell you the legend that is attached to them?"

"No, he did not tell me the legend."

"I wonder if he knows it . . ." Diana said thoughtfully. "He was a child when he came here, and I myself did not hear the tale until I was older." She drew her horse closer to Julie. "Shall I tell it to you?"

"Please, I should really like to hear it," Julie said.

"Well . . ." Diana leaned back in her saddle. "Legend has it that these rocks were once the heads of giants—a man and a woman, who loved deeply—as Shakespeare puts it, 'not wisely but too well.' They were each married to someone else, and one day when they were in the midst of their guilty rapture, their angry spouses discovered them. They called upon the gods to avenge them.

"In those days, the Vikings ruled these lands, and it was Thor, with his hammer, who took vengeance upon the guilty lovers. He struck their heads from their bodies —but being immortal, they could not die and their two heads remained placed one on top of the other, lips against lips, in an eternal kiss. But of course, robbed of their bodies, they found little joy in that particular communion.

"Then the Norsemen were driven away and their gods went with them. The Christ child came to these shores and one day he was wandering over this bit of land, and seeing the poor giants, he took pity on their agony and turned them into stone—and there they remain as a horrid example of what can happen to a pair of adulterers."

"Oh dear." Julie shivered. "That is a dreadful story."

"You do not believe that they received their just deserts, Julie?"

"The punishment seems rather severe," Julie commented.

"In the old days, unfaithful lovers and whoring wives

were taken rather more seriously than now. More than one outraged husband walled his wife up in the castle," Diana said. "But come, let me show you the coastline and then we will ride to the Logan stones."

It was a wonderful view, wonderful and wild as a rising wind drove the sea against the shore. The wind seemed to have gathered some of its foam and was tossing it against Julie's face in the form of tiny stinging pinpricks. From the path that ran close to the edge of the cliffs she could see a long line of rocky coast with its coves and inlets. There were small fishing boats bouncing on the waters far beyond the breakers, and above them the sea gulls wheeled and screamed, lighting on masts or diving toward the decks in search of food. The wind was blowing harder now, and it was on the tip of Julie's tongue to suggest that they ride back. Indeed, given Diana's awareness of her supposed illness, she ought to have suggested it herself, Julie reasoned. However, compassion and consideration were not the girl's strong points, and to give her the benefit of the doubt, she seemed very proud of this wild country and eager to share this pride with a visitor.

"We will go this way!" Diana called back. "And you must take care not to ride too near the cliff's edge." She wheeled her mount around.

Julie, following her, called, "Is it very far to your stones?"

"No, not very . . . you cannot see them from here, but once we have rounded the bend in the road, we will be in sight of our stony lovers."

They had gone some little way before they reached that aforementioned bend in the road. Julie guessed that Diana, used as she was to riding through the area, was not a very good judge of distance. Very likely, once she had set her mind on a given goal, reaching it was all that mattered. And that, Julie thought with a little shiver, might describe her discouraging of poor Sir Anthony, who stood in the way of her aspirations to be a countess. However, she did not want to dwell on that. She urged her horse forward, and rounding the bend, she saw them, two immense rocks, seemingly precariously balanced, the one on top of the other, swaying slightly in the wind . . . and yes, there was a definite resemblance to a pair of human heads frozen forever in a travesty of a kiss.

Dismounting, Diana tied her horse to a nearby tree, and coming back to Julie, who had pull her horse to a stop, she said, "Come, you must see them from all angles, and you cannot do that unless you are on foot."

"Very well." Julie slipped out of her saddle, and winding the reins around her hand, followed Diana's example and tied her horse to another tree. The wind was still blowing a gale as they walked toward the rocks. Moving ahead of Julie, Diana circled them, cocking her head and looking at them from different angles. "I think," she called, "that you can see them best from here. Come, and you will agree with me, I know."

Following Diana, Julie glanced down and saw that they were very near the ocean. The waves looked particularly wild. They pounded against the shore in an almost manic assault, and sliding out, revealed jagged rocks, their edges sharp as spear tips. Near those perilously balanced stones, the cliff sloped down to a rocky ledge half-covered with moss, and then below it was a sheer drop to the shore. Julie shuddered. Though there were at least three or even four feet of earth between her and the cliff's edge, she was visited by an image of herself plummeting down, down, down to the impaling rocks below.

"Be careful where you step," Diana cautioned unnecessarily. "The ground is hard here—but closer to the cliff's edge, it might be soft from the recent rains."

"I think," Julie said, "that I would as lief see them from here."

"Oh, come." Diana laughed. "I did not mean to scare you. It is really quite safe. Look at me. I am much taller than you and I have been coming here since I was a child. I can assure you that I have never fallen, and nor will you—but if you are afraid, you had best remain where you are."

Julie heard mockery in Diana's tones and read it in her gaze. "I am not afraid," she said indignantly. "But what, in fact, is there to see?"

"Not very much, actually," Diana said kindly. "You are probably right. You would be safer standing where you are now than on the other side."

There was contempt in Diana's eyes . . . and would she describe their excursion to Richard in a way that must emphasize Julie's cowardice? Julie gritted her teeth, and staying close to the rocks, edged her way slowly toward Diana. However, once she had looked up at the massive outlines of those frozen heads from Diana's vantage point, she was surprised. She did not find them nearly as impressive as they had been from the far side. From having half-human outlines, they seemed now to have become no more than massive rocks. Evidently Diana's imagination was more active than her own.

"Well?" Diana asked challengingly. "Do you not agree?"

"I am not sure that I do," Julie responded. "I think I prefer them from the other side."

"Really?" Diana appeared surprised. "Evidently you see something there that I do not."

"Or"— Julie managed a smile—"you see something *here* that I do not."

"Well, then," Diana said, "since you are probably uncomfortable here, let us look at them from the other side. Be careful where you step, now."

"I will," Julie assured her, shuddering as a long stream of water plunged against the cliffside. If one were to talk of shapes—it reminded her of a grasping hand.

Behind her, Diana gave a little exclamation of fright, and as Julie looked over her shoulder, the girl slipped and fell against her, loosening Julie's hold on the rocks and sending her backward.

With a gasp of terror, Julie found herself slipping. She reached out wildly, but her hands closed on air, and then she was over the cliff's edge. Clutching wildly yet again, she managed to seize a vine. As her fingers closed on it, she felt earth beneath her, and staring down, saw that she was standing on that rocky ledge she had seen earlier. She pressed herself against the cliffside, her fingers digging into the damp rocky earth. Above her Diana shrieked. She had heard that sound before, she knew. It was still echoing through her fear-benumbed brain.

The sound of the tumultuous waves was loud in her ears. The vines and the rocks of the cliffside pressed against her body. After a moment she dared to look upward and found Diana staring down at her, mouth open and eyes wide with terror.

"Julie," she called. "Oh God, you are alive. Let me see if . . . if I can reach you." She edged nearer the cliff, and lying flat on her stomach, reached down her arm— but it extended to a point at least two feet above Julie's head. "I cannot . . . reach you," she cried. "Help . . . I must fetch help." Foolishly she added, "Stay where you are. I will be back soon . . . as soon as possible."

Julie could not respond. Her heart was beating in her throat. She could only watch while Diana edged back, mouthing words of encouragement. Then she was gone, and a few moments later Julie heard something very like laughter borne on that cold biting wind—laughter and the hoofbeats of a swift horse diminishing into the distance.

10

Diana rode on her way rejoicing. Her plan, evolved through a sleepless night, had worked so simply, so seamlessly, that she could hardly credit her good luck. In her mind's eye she could envision little Julie waiting there, waiting, waiting, waiting, until her hands grew numb, until the strong sea winds, increasing in velocity, tore at her, and she, stiff with cold, must needs loosen her clutch on the vines and on the chill earth beneath them and plummet to her death on the jagged rocks below.

Her hope had been for a swifter demise, but Julie had fallen on the ledge, and that meant her agony would be prolonged. She would grow weaker and weaker as she screamed for help, the help that would never come.

That was the vision that entertained Diana and kept her horse to a trot . . . but she had not gone very far when fright took the place of exaltation.

She and Julie had gone riding together, and now she was returning alone. She could explain that they had become separated—but the tale would not hold water. When she returned her horse not even lathered, she might be blamed for not looking for the girl, and she might even be accused of complicity if anything were to happen to Julie. . . . Perhaps it had happened already! Had the winds increased? They were rising.

Suddenly an image of Ellen arose in Diana's mind.

She had once lost her temper with the abigail, had scratched and pummeled her, and chasing her into the hall, had tried to push her down the stairs! The girl had left her service just as that French witch had done, and for far less reason. Yet, would it matter what Ellen said? Possibly. Sir Nigel had comforted the frightened abigail, had given her a large sum of money as well, and when extra servants were needed, he had always hired her. Diana's father himself might be suspicious regarding Julie's fall. There had been other incidents. . . . It occurred to Diana that he had been surprised and pleased that she had wanted to go riding with Julie. Had he previously imagined that she had developed one of her "spites," as he called them, against the young woman?

Fear was a hard stone in her throat. She must cover her tracks, summon help and hope, hope, hope that the little witch had fallen to her death. Shattered on the rocks, she would not be so appealing to Richard and Anthony!

She urged her horse into a canter and then into a full gallop. A rumble overhead brought her attention to the sky. There were more clouds—soon they would be massing together and the rain would come. It might begin at any time! It might begin well before they reached Julie. She could delay a little longer. No, better not . . . but if Julie were rescued, could she not accuse her. . . ? No, for who could say it had not been an accident? Not Julie, certainly! She brought her crop down on her horse's back, and reaching the stableyard still at full gallop, her horse exhausted and quite satisfactorily lathered, she waited only until she could pull him in before throwing herself off and blurting out her tale to the stablehands. Then she ran into the house, and coming into the main hall breathless, asked a passing servant where she might find her father or the earl.

"I am here, Diana." The earl appeared on the first landing of the stairs. He added as he started down, "Where is Julie? I thought you went riding together."

"She . . ." She hesitated a split second, her thoughts battering at her head. She did not want to tell Richard, of all people . . . fearing that if she did, he might possibly suspect . . . but again, how could he? "I . . . I have told them at the . . . the stables. Julie . . ."

A look of anger mixed with suspicion clouded his eyes. He ran down the remaining steps, and confronting her, put his hands on her shoulders. "What has happened? Something has happened to her, has it not? What?" He shook her slightly. "Tell me."

His hands were hard on her shoulders and he had shaken her. "You're hurting me, Richard!" she cried indignantly.

His grip did not relax. "Tell me what happened, Diana."

"The cliffs . . . I thought to . . . to show her the Kissing Rocks . . . I accidently fell against her, and she went over."

His face went white. "You . . . you are not telling me that she . . . that she . . ." His voice broke, and, his fingers pressing into her arms like talons, he shook her again, and much harder, as he cried, "She's not dead?"

"No, let me go, damn you." She tried to wrench free of him, but to no avail. "She is not dead, Richard. She fell on the ledge . . ."

"She is unconscious?"

"No, she . . . there's nothing the matter with her. She took no hurt, only I could not reach her to get her off the ledge. I came to summon help, and as I said, I told the stable lads."

"The ledge in this weather and with the winds rising and rain in the air!" he said in utter horror. Turning on his heel, he ran out of the house, slamming the front

door behind him. Staring at it and hearing the rever-
berations of that slam, Diana realized that she had
known from the very first how he felt about the woman
he had dared to pass off as his friend's wife!

"If only . . ." she muttered, her fury rising again as in
her mind's eye she saw Julie's body impaled on those
jagged rocks.

"It would serve her right," she muttered.

Then she shook her head as her anger, draining from
her, left sheer horror in its wake. As had happened so
often after her violent outbursts, remorse followed
quickly. She dashed out of the house and was at the
stable in minutes. As she started toward the gates, they
were thrown open, and the earl, mounted on his horse,
swept past her, narrowly missing her. Then, mixed with
the thunder of his horse's hooves, was an ominous
rumble overhead. Diana felt a splatter of rain on her
cheek. It was what she had hoped must happen—given
the alternate darkening and lightening of the sky—but
now she did not want it to occur. She started forward,
only to leap aside once more as Matt and Ethan, two of
the stablehands, rode after the earl. Then she rushed in
to reclaim her horse.

As she mounted, she was joined by her father.
"What's all the furor?" he demanded. "Where is
Richard going with Matt and Ethan?"

"Julie . . . she fell near the Kissing Rocks."

He stared at her in horror. "She's not dead!"

"No . . . she fell on the ledge." Diana put spurs to her
horse and rode after the others.

The rain was beginning to fall, and Julie, clinging to
the vines, was cold with terror. Her fingers were so stiff,
and the high winds whipped about her, tearing at her.
The spray from the moiling waters dashing at the rocks
below had drenched her garments. They clung clammily

to her body, and they, too, were cold, as cold as cerements. She shuddered at the analogy.

They might well be her shroud—but she would not lie in a grave; the rocks below would be briefly her bier, and then those raging waters would carry her out to . . . far out . . . They wanted her. They had been earlier robbed of their prey . . . Richard had foiled them, had brought her on his ship, out of their reach, but they were not to be foiled. They were strong and angry, as strong and angry as the woman who had helped them to claim her. Diana, whose laughter had echoed in her ears as she rode triumphantly away. There was really no reason to cling here so desperately, and as desperately pray for rescue!

Diana would not tell anyone where she was, and her hands were already numb. She would not be able to hang on much longer, but she could not, would not let go. Death waited below, but she did not want to die. Yet, were she to remain here much longer, there would be no choice. Diana had said she would fetch help, but that was a lie, a lie, a lie. . . . She had brought her here for only one purpose, and she had achieved that purpose.

What would she tell them? What *could* she tell them? What did it matter? No one would believe that it was anything but an accident—no one save Ellen, who had begged her not to go. . . . Ellen might guess the truth.

"Julie, thank God!"

She looked up, the cry ringing in her ears, and there he was. "Richard," she breathed, staring into his fear-distorted face.

"Hold on, my dearest, hold on," he counseled. "I will have you up shortly."

"But," she protested, "you must not think of trying to fetch me. It is too dangerous."

"Hush, my love, just hold on tightly, tightly." He

moved back, and rising, turned toward Matt. "You and Ethan secure the rope to this tree. I think it will hold, do you not?"

"Aye, your lordship." Matt examined the trunk of the weather-stunted pine. "It will."

"Richard . . ." Sir Nigel had arrived. "Is she . . . ?"

"She's not . . . ?" Diana rode up.

"She is still down there on the ledge," the earl said hoarsely. "Providence was kind and she . . . but there's no time to waste in explanations." He turned to Matt. "Have you fastened the rope to the tree?"

"That we have, your lordship. Ethan's just securing it now." He turned back, saying, "Another knot, Ethan. That ought to do it." Matt faced the earl again. "It will hold, your lordship."

"Are you sure?" he demanded. "It must bear the weight of two."

"There won't be any trouble. It's strong rope, and I am not heavy, your lordship."

"You are not going, Matt. I am bringing Julie up," the earl said. "Is it strong enough to bear my weight?"

"But, your lordship"—Ethan came forward—"it's best one of us goes."

"Richard," Diana shrilled, "you cannot go down there. You . . . you'll be killed."

He barely glanced at her. "I am not afraid. The rope, please, Matt, will it hold?"

"Yes, your lordship, I am sure it will, but—"

"Then wind it around me and make another of your knots."

"There's not much of a foothold, your lordship."

"No matter, I am used to . . . God!" he exclaimed as a sudden gust of windblown rain splattered against his face. "There's no time to lose . . . the rain's bound to get heavier, and soon. The rope, Matt. Hurry."

The stablehand was at his side in a trice. He tied the

rope around the earl's waist. As he did, Sir Nigel moved forward. "Be careful, Richard, some of those rocks are loose."

"You must not go!" Diana cried again.

As if he had not heard her, the earl tested the knots. "They seem strong enough," he said calmly. "Come, lads, lower me. The ledge is wide enough so that I can find a foothold on it. Once I have Julie in my arms, start pulling as fast as you can . . . it is not a long distance, thank God."

The wind was increasing. It whipped Julie's skirts about her and tore at her hair. It seemed to have developed hands, strong hands that wanted to pull her down—while her own hands were turning to ice. She could not hold on much longer—but she must hold on, because Richard was there. Richard had come to rescue her—but how could he manage a rescue from this precarious ledge? She looked up and saw Diana staring down at her, her face white.

"Hold on, Julie," she said through stiff lips. "Hold on, for God's sake!"

Then suddenly, there was Richard, a rope knotted about his waist, crawling over the cliff. "Hold on, my sweetest," he called.

"Oh, no, no, please, no, Richard," Julie screamed. "You . . . it's too dangerous. You must not—"

"Be silent," he admonished.

He had been lowered almost to the ledge when a strong gust of wind struck him, and to Julie's horror, he swung out over the jagged rocks, over the lashing, wind-driven waves. She shrieked, and there were cries from above as well. Then there were arms around her and she heard Richard yell hoarsely, "I have her . . . I have her fast . . . now pull, pull, pull!"

The wind was their enemy. It howled and whistled about them as, momentarily dangling together in the air, they were raised up, up, up until there was earth beneath them, until they fell together on that earth, the earl's arms still around Julie, his voice in her ear. "My darling, my dearest love, you are safe! Oh, my love, you are safe."

"Richard . . ." She trembled against him. "And you are safe. I was so frightened for you, so frightened."

"Thank God!" Sir Nigel spoke gruffly. "There was a moment when I feared . . ." He stared down at Richard, his expression half-relieved, half-stern. "We must speak . . . but now, certainly, is not the time."

Diana, staring at them, said nothing. She went back to her horse, and mounting it, rode swiftly away.

Richard, with Julie before him in his saddle, his arms around her waist and his chin resting on her head, rode swiftly back. He had not spoken and neither had she. Her recent brush with death and her return to a life that was suddenly filled with love had left her wondering if, after all, she had fallen from the ledge and been magically transported to heaven, but of course that was ridiculous! She was alive because Richard had miraculously appeared to save her from death—just as he had when she thought herself in peril of drowning. The sea, she thought with a shudder, had every reason to be angry—being twice deprived of its prey.

"Are you cold, my love?" Richard asked solicitously, his arms tightening about her.

"No, not in the least . . ."

"You should be. You are wet through."

"How could I be cold when you are holding me so closely?" she asked reasonably.

He dropped a kiss on her head. "I hope I am not crushing you."

"No, I am most comfortable, Richard."

"As am I, my dearest love."

"Oh, Richard, do you really love me?" she murmured.

"Can you doubt it?" he asked huskily.

"No."

"Then why ask such foolish, such ridiculous questions?" he chided lovingly.

"Because I want to hear the answers. I have loved you for such a long time, Richard."

"And I have loved you so much, so very much, Julie. My heart was cold within me at the thought of marrying Diana. But now, no one can hold me to that promise, which was never mine, but, as I told you, of my parents' arranging. And I think now I could not have gone through with it . . . each day seemed more difficult than the one before, each day, each hour . . . because you see, my love, no man can function without his heart. You are my heart, my Julie. You are my life."

"Oh, Richard, you are mine," she said, nestling against him. "Still . . ."

"Still . . . what, my love?"

"I wonder if, after all, I am not dreaming."

"If you are dreaming, so am I," he said huskily, and dropped another kiss on her hair. Then he urged his horse forward. "If we are not to catch a quinsy, we must hurry back and you must get out of those wet clothes immediately. We will have a lot of traveling ahead of us in the next two days."

Sir Nigel, his eyes cold and accusing, sat at his desk in the library, looking not unlike a justice of the peace confronting a captured poacher, the earl thought uncomfortably.

"Richard," he said heavily, "I think . . ." He paused. "I really cannot find words to express what I think of a man who brings his mistress to the home of the girl he has promised to marry, and with that wedding imminent."

The earl rose to his feet. In a tone as cold as that of his host he said, "She is not my mistress, but—"

"But," Sir Nigel interrupted, "I would wager a monkey that she is not the widow of—"

"No, sir," it was the earl's turn to interrupt, "she is neither my mistress nor Christopher's widow, but I pray you will let me explain."

"You need not pray for that, Richard," Sir Nigel said sarcastically. "I am quite anxious to hear that explanation."

He listened closely while the earl, moving back and forth across the room, recounted his meeting with Julie and their subsequent adventures. "The fact," he concluded, "that she came here under false pretenses was purely at my insistence. She did not want to come. She was determined to get back to Brighton. However, I was fearful that she would be accosted at every turn in the road. You see, Sir Nigel, she is totally unaware of her great beauty."

"Ummmm." Sir Nigel stared at him. "I see something else, too, Richard. I see that you were in love with her even before you brought her here."

"I *liked* her," the earl emphasized. "Perhaps, unknown even to myself, I more than liked her, but I was quite determined to abide by my promise, or, rather, by the arrangements made by my late parents. If this had not happened . . . But when I saw her in such peril, I knew that if she were to . . . to die, I would not want to live."

Sir Nigel was silent a moment, staring down at his desk and absently fingering a crystal paperweight. Finally he said slowly, "You are very frank, Richard, but are you being very practical?"

"Practical, sir?"

"I know you have very little feeling for my daughter, but I have investigated your affairs. I know that your pockets are 'to let,' as the saying goes."

"Sir!" The earl rose swiftly to his feet. "I think we have nothing more—"

"Let me have my say," Sir Nigel interrupted. "You may not love my daughter, but her dowry is large. I am a warm man and everything I own will be hers when I die. I would be willing to settle all your debts if you were to decide that, after all, you would honor the wishes of your late parents and marry Diana."

"Sir Nigel"—the earl drew himself up—"were Diana as rich as King Midas, I would not marry her, feeling as I do about Julie. I have made up my mind. I will sell my estates, and I might even move to Canada, where we have some acreage."

Sir Nigel rose to his feet. "You would not do that!" he exclaimed. "Your lands have been in your family since the eleventh century!"

The earl nodded. "My lands would mean very little to me without Julie. My life would mean very little too. I realized how little this afternoon. I could never make your daughter happy." His face darkened. "But now, when we both, I think, know that Diana was instrumental in—"

"Richard!" Sir Nigel took a step forward, his hands clenched. "I do not wish to call you out—so I charge you, say no more. Diana is and has always been . . . impulsive. She . . . But we will not discuss this matter. I . . . I accept what you have told me, and I do like you. I expect that I also admire your purpose, so let me bid you and . . . the young woman who will be your wife, Godspeed."

"I thank you, Sir Nigel," the earl said steadily. "And now, I must beg that you excuse me. I want to see how Julie is faring."

"You are excused, Richard." Sir Nigel shook his head and sighed deeply. "I wish . . . But no matter. Get you to your love, and I hope that for all our sakes, she will not be stricken with a quinsy. It is not my way to speed the parting guest, but on this occasion I would think that the sooner you could make ready to leave, the better it would be for all concerned.''

"I am entirely in agreement, Sir Nigel," the earl said. "I will bid you good afternoon and . . . farewell." He hurriedly left the room, and taking the stairs in several bounds, he knocked on Julie's chamber door.

Ellen opened it, looking so grave that his heart plummeted. "How is she?" he demanded.

"She is bathed, she is dressed, and she is quite ready to leave—if you should desire it," said a lilting voice behind the abigail.

"And I have told her that after her ordeal on that cliff with all those winds buffeting her, and her wet to the skin, she ought not to think of leaving, especially with the weather turning so chill," Ellen said concernedly as she stepped back to allow him to enter.

The earl, looking down into Julie's smiling face, put his hands on her shoulders. "I think she is right . . . even if we go only as far as an inn in Helston, we must be away from here. I will have my clothes packed immediately."

"Oh, I am glad." Julie clapped her hands. "Will you always be so accommodating, Richard?" she added lovingly.

"All the days of my life, my dearest," he said softly. Unmindful of the abigail, he caught her in his arms, covering her face with kisses.

The inn was small, and Julie, sitting in a cozy private parlor bespoken by the earl, looked out on the distant harbor, where, on the following morning, they would be boarding the yacht. She loosed a quavering breath, wishing that they might have sailed on the night tide. It would be a long, long time before she would feel comfortable on the craggy shores of Cornwall, a long time before she would forget the terror on the cliffs—or

Diana's laughter echoing in her ears as she urged her horse into a gallop, leaving Julie to press herself against the vine-covered boulders.

She shook her head. She must try to put that terrible ordeal out of her mind, and think instead of Richard. She wondered where he had gone. He had spoken about an errand. What manner of errand might he have in this town? She had no answers to that question, and she was really too weary to speculate on it. Indeed, she was too weary to think of anything, and yet images continued to dart through her brain, vivid images filling her mind's eye. She saw herself on that narrow ledge with the greedy waters below, stretching out their foamy arms . . . some of them *had* resembled arms, or, rather, tentacles . . . a leviathan rising from the depths. . . . She must not dwell on that either.

"Where is Richard?" she murmured, and loosed a long sigh of pure happiness.

He loved her, had loved her for a long time, he had told her, and would love her for the rest of his life—and she had been able to tell him how much she loved him. And he had kissed her hands . . . and when they were in the coach, he had drawn her into his arms and continued to kiss her. She had felt very shy at first—but then a passion she had never experienced engulfed her. Thinking about it now, she felt her cheeks burn . . . and why was he taking such a long time on his errand?

She rose and went to the window, looking down on the narrow cobblestoned street. It was a lovely sight . . . not because the old houses and tiny shops were beautiful, but because they were not the gardens where, if one went walking, one would meet Diana, jealous Diana, who had seen her with Sir Anthony and with Richard and had concluded that she was trying to annex them both. Julie had discussed this theory with Richard and found him in agreement.

Astonishingly, he had said, "There were times when I

wanted to strangle Sir Anthony, times when I thought you had a *tendre* for him. He wanted you."

"I cannot agree with you," she had said. "I am of the opinion that he only wanted to make Diana jealous."

"Oh, Julie, Julie, Julie," he had sighed, "can you not understand the spell you cast over us poor defenseless men? You are an enchantress . . . a Circe, no, not a Circe, for she knew all too well the effect she had on her hapless victims. You, my love, are an innocent."

"I think you must be funning me," she had chided.

"No, my dearest, I am telling you the truth. Can you not understand why I plucked you from the coach and brought you with me? I wanted to protect you and . . . and instead . . ." His voice had broken. "Oh, Julie, instead, I brought you perilously close to the mouth of hell . . . so close that I nearly lost you."

"I was so frightened for *you*," she had said. "When that rope swung out over those raging waters and—"

"But we are here." He had closed her mouth with a kiss.

"Julie . . ."

She started and looked up. He had returned at last and he was gazing at her so lovingly that her heart began to beat heavily. Indeed, she felt well-nigh overwhelmed by feelings for which she had no name. She said breathlessly, "Oh, Richard, at last you are here."

"I am sorry I was so long. But now all is arranged, and never have I been so happy for those circumstances that made me an earl. We will not have to wait another day, not another hour, my Julie."

"Wait . . . for what . . . I do not understand," she said confusedly.

"For me to make you my wife, my dearest. As a peer of the realm, I was able to obtain a special license from the local bishop. Come with me, Julie, come and be married. Will you?"

"Oh, yes, Richard." She held out her hands and felt

them seized. Bringing first one and then the other to his lips, he drew her up and led her out of the room.

Julie stood in front of the little mirror in their chamber at the inn. She was brushing her hair. Behind her in the mirror she saw reflected the wide four-poster bed, its covers pulled back to reveal snowy sheets and plump pillows. Soon she would be sharing it with the man who was her husband. . . . Her *husband*?

To think of that was to remember the setting sun sending its rays through the stained-glass windows of Helston's church, throwing a pattern of reds and blues on the benign face of the old minister who had married them. If he had been surprised to find a bride clad in black save for the lacy white shawl the earl had been able to purchase just before he returned to the inn, he had given no evidence of it, and neither had his wife or the gentle young curate who had acted as witnesses. It was the curate who had hurried to the choir loft to play a hymn as they moved out of the church.

Now, arrayed in her peignoir and nightgown, she glanced once at the bed and shivered slightly. Against her will, she was remembering that terrible night when Edwin had tossed her into bed and, a very short time later, left her weeping from the pain he had inflicted on her. She did not *want* to be afraid of Richard. She was not afraid of him, yet . . . Edwin had seemed so mild until their wedding night.

"Passion changes a man," her sister Eliza had told her with a sigh that Julie had perfectly understood after her horrid session with Edwin.

Would passion change Richard?

She wanted to believe that it would not. Still . . . Her thoughts fled. The door was opening, and Richard, clad in a long white nightshirt very like the one Edwin had worn, stood on the threshold.

"My love," he said, and in common with Edwin,

crossed the room in what seemed a single stride.

She rose, her heart beating or, rather, pounding in her throat as he caught her in his arms. He held her against him, kissing her in a way he never had before. It was an invading kiss and yet she found it exciting rather than frightening. Then he lifted her, and holding her against his chest, carried her to the bed. Edwin had also carried her to the bed and had flung her down as if she were a sack of meal. Subsequently he had thrown himself on top of her, unmindful of her frightened cries.

Richard placed her gently in the bed and slid in beside her, putting his arms around her and dropping gentle little kisses on her face and throat—yet gentle as they were, they were filling her with an excitement and a desire she had never experienced before.

She wanted . . . But she was not sure what she wanted. Yet she knew instinctively that before the evening was at an end, she would know. She shyly moved closer to him and then tensed as he gently eased her nightgown down. That had happened before, only Edwin had wrenched it off, tearing the delicate fabric. . . .

There was nothing violent in Richard's movements, and Julie found she could help him, wriggling out of the gown and then lying close against him, against his own nakedness, and knowing that it was right that they should be together in this way. . . .

He was murmuring little words of love and she dared to respond, dared to press against him, to open her mouth for his kisses . . . while his caresses grew more passionate, a passion that invaded her as well . . . until at last it seemed to her that her very soul had left her body and was floating in the air beside that of her lover . . . floating ecstatically into a state she had never dreamed existed. . . .

Later, lying beside him, she knew, at long last, the entire meaning of love.

11

The Earl and Countess of Aylsford were arguing softly as their post chaise brought them up the long drive to the house.

His lordship regarded the building with an anger which had, however, nothing to do with its impressive facade. His eyes shifted to his wife's determined face. "I do not want you to see them alone, Julie," he protested.

"I must . . . at first," she responded. "It is possible that they were merely concerned, you know."

"I do not know, and from all you have told me . . ." He shook his head. "I cannot understand such cupidity! Rather than being overjoyed that you brought such largess into the family coffers, they stood ready to imprison you."

"I do not expect they would have imprisoned me," she said.

"No," he responded sarcastically. "They would have shunted you out to one or another country house and watched your every move. Or they would have tried to force you to sign away your inheritance in return for your freedom." He regarded her with something akin to wonder in his gaze. "Fifty thousand pounds! Men have murdered each other for a fraction of that. Lord, it seems incredible. And here I was ready to leave for Canada when you told me—but I do not know why I was surprised that brilliance should walk hand in hand with beauty. I knew you were intelligent and eminently sensible—but to possess such gifts . . . again, I say I do not deserve you."

"Richard," Julie said firmly, "I beg you will not be so nonsensical. What would my life have been without you?"

"Or mine without you, dearest. Still"—he looked at her concernedly—"I think I must go with you."

"You will not be far away, and if they grow difficult, you may, of course, rescue me. Allow me this little . . . may we call it a play or, possibly, a farce? If they react as I expect, I fear it will be the latter. I hope, however, that they will be pleased that I did not drown."

"If they are not, may heaven strike—" He stopped as Julie put a hand over his mouth.

"If they are not"—she smiled—"then they will have already received their . . . er . . . due."

"If you are talking about disappointment, I insist that they have not," he said angrily. "When I think . . ." He paused as the carriage drew to a stop.

"We will soon know what we must think," Julie murmured.

The elderly butler, after the first shock of seeing Julie and her husband, still looked as if he were about to cry. However, with what appeared to be a mighty effort of will, he pulled himself together and listened closely to Julie's instructions. He nodded several times and then said, "Miss Julie . . . oh, dear Miss Julie, an' lookin' so bloomin'n beautiful. An' 'ere Lucy were tellin' us all you was dead! Oh, Miss Julie, she'll be that glad! She were fair beside 'erself when she come back."

Julie smiled affectionately at the old man. "I am glad to hear that she did come back. I expect she'll be with her mother?"

"Yes, miss . . . milady." The butler looked at the earl.

"Now, Price," Julie said, "you do know what you are to do when the time comes. I will stamp my foot twice, so you'd best remain in earshot. His lordship will be just beyond the door."

"I will do as you say, Miss Julie." A conspiratorial gleam lit his faded eyes. "An' 'twill serve 'em right, it will." He regarded her anxiously. "But mind you take care. Mr. Raymond, 'e's not like yer father, and 'er . . ." He shook his head.

"I know, Price," Julie said. "Times change. But no matter, you may announce me."

"I still think . . ." the earl muttered.

"Please," she protested softly. "You did promise, Richard."

"Very well," he whispered reluctantly. "But if . . ." He paused as the butler, having moved into the drawing room, held the door ajar as he made his startling announcement in his usual grave, uninflected tones.

"Good God!" Julie heard her brother cry explosively. "You'll never be telling me that she is . . . is not . . ."

The earl moved back toward the outer door, and Julie waited to hear no more. She came into the drawing room. "Yes, it is I, Raymond, and no, I am not dead."

Sir Raymond stared at her incredulously, his face paling. Coming to her side, he said weakly, "Good God, Julie, it is you. We thought . . ."

"Yes," she responded coldly, now that he had made no move to embrace her. "Judging from what the bank manager told me when I went to withdraw money from my account, you were there ahead of me, seeking to seize possession of my funds in the belief that I was dead. I expect you must have received that notion from Lucy, and, again, it must have been she who informed you I was in Brighton."

He appeared to be momentarily without words. Then

he said, "Even before your abigail told us that you had
been living in Brighton, we were sure, from what you
said to us on the day that you deemed it necessary to . . .
to leave this house by stealth, that Brighton was your
destination. Had we not been so preoccupied with
matters attendant upon Father's death, we would have
gone there earlier."

"To bring me back?" Julie asked mockingly.

She received a cold, disapproving look from her
brother. "Yes, to bring you back. I am now the head of
the family. I stand in the place of Father and I am sure
that I speak for him when I say that he would never have
countenanced your living alone in such a place."

"He did countenance it. He told me to go," she
retorted. "Even on his deathbed, he made me promise
that I would change none of our plans."

"His wits were obviously wandering . . . that was
evident in his . . . disposition of his . . . er, worldly
goods," Sir Raymond said coolly. "Had he been in his
right mind . . . But enough. Where have you been all
this time?"

"Before I answer that—" she began.

"You will answer my question," he interrupted icily.
"Where were you, Julie, and what have you been
doing?" His eyes wandered over her gown, a white silk
with three rows of ruffles at the hem. Over it she had
draped a lavender silk shawl, one of Richard's many
gifts, and she was carrying a matching reticule. Her
bonnet was decorated with a small white ostrich plume
and around her neck was a pearl choker, also Richard's
gift. She was well aware that she looked expensively
turned-out and guessed that her brother must imagine
that she had bought the ensemble and the jewelry
herself. On looking at him, she found his gaze hot with
resentment. "I see that you have lost no time in
abandoning your mourning," he said accusingly.

"It was Papa's oft-expressed wish that I not wear mourning. White and lavender, however, are considered mourning shades. That is aside from the point, Raymond. To return to my supposed demise. I have always had the impression that one must wait seven years to establish the fact that a disappearance is tantamount to a death. You did not wait so much as a fortnight, I am told."

"What were we to think?" he responded angrily. "Your abigail came to us in hysterics to tell us that a young woman of your description was seen in a rowboat in the midst of a tempest and that the boat washed up in pieces the following day. Logically, we assumed that you had been drowned."

"That still does not explain . . ." she began, and paused as Lady Carleton, looking harried, entered hastily. She came to a dead stop, staring at Julie even more incredulously than had her husband. There was no warmth in her tones as she said sharply, "You! Where have you been hiding?"

Julie regarded her sister-in-law coolly. "I think that is no concern of yours, Alicia. Suffice to say that I am alive, I am well, and I am in command of my resources. I have written to acquaint Mr. Soames of that fact, and one of the reasons I am here is to save you any further embarrassment on that count. The other—"

"I demand to know where you have been!" Sir Raymond interrupted.

"I would say that from the looks of her, she has found herself a rich lover . . . or did he find you?" Lady Carleton demanded contemptuously. "It would not be the first time!"

Julie drew herself up. "I understand that you also put a Bow Street Runner on my trail, as if, indeed, I were a common criminal! That, too, was told to me in Brighton when I returned. I have been half-inclined to prefer charges against you, not only for these actions but also for your reprehensible efforts to detain me here against my will. Yet, in spite of that, I was ready to give you the benefit of the doubt . . . to hope that it was anxiety rather than cupidity that moved you in that direction."

"Whatever we did, we were in our rights," Lady Carleton snapped.

"Your . . . rights?" Julie repeated incredulously. "What rights are those, pray? I am of age and competent."

"I disagree," her brother said icily. "You have already proved yourself an adulteress and it is my opinion that you should and must be restrained from bringing more ignominy and infamy down upon our family."

"Restrained?" Julie echoed. "I think not. You, my dear Raymond, have no jurisdiction over my actions."

"To the contrary," Lady Carleton retorted. "We have every right in the world. Your brother is head of the family . . . But enough. You were not very wise to come here unescorted, my dear Julie. We do not know where you have been, and it is of little matter now. In the future, your whereabouts will not be so difficult to discover."

"Will you keep me under lock and key, then?" Julie demanded sarcastically.

"If it is necessary—" Lady Carleton began.

"I think," Julie interrupted, "that you will not be able to make good that ridiculous threat. I am not in the same position that I was when I was forced to climb out of my window merely because I had inherited the fifty thousand pounds that was my portion of the sum I helped my father realize."

"That is a madness in itself!" Lady Carleton snapped. "Tell anyone that tale, my dear Julie, and they will have no difficulty agreeing that you should be sent to Bedlam!"

"I am finding this conversation more and more distasteful," Julie retorted. "I think we must bring it to a close. I will take my leave of you now . . ." She turned and started for the door, only to be confronted by her brother. "Let me pass!" she commanded.

"You are not leaving here again, Julie," he said coldly.

With a coldness that matched his own, she repeated, "Let me pass. You have no right to detain me."

"We can and will both detain and restrain you." Lady Carleton stepped forward to seize Julie's arm in a viselike grip. "Your former husband will give his testimony regarding your reprehensible actions before your shocking divorce. He will mention your confused mental state, and I think you will not find a court in the land that will not uphold us. You are clearly mad! And it is a cunning madness that drove you to exercise undue influence on a dying old man, you little wretch! Indeed, I would not have put it past you to have hastened his death in order to feather your nest!"

"Alicia!" Julie gasped. Given her reception by Raymond and his wife, she had expected to be showered with invective. However, Lady Carleton had exceeded these expectations. She had actually accused her of murdering her own father.

"Good God, I would not have credited it, my dearest!" the earl said explosively as he strode into the room. Reaching the two women, he caught Lady Carleton's wrist, and wrenching it from Julie's arm, he thrust her back roughly.

"Damn you, who are you!" Sir Raymond demanded as his wife screamed with a mixture of surprise and pain. He leapt at the earl and went staggering back at a hearty thrust from the newcomer.

Turning to Julie, the earl added a trifle breathlessly, "I had hoped that you were exaggerating, my dearest love, but I see that you were far too kind."

"That was not the signal!" Julie raised her voice over the angry protests from her brother and his wife. "But, after all, Richard, I am very glad you came when you did. Their combined malevolence was beginning to be very wearisome." She turned accusing eyes on her brother's flushed countenance. "It was also extremely depressing—suggesting that blood is not thicker than water, after all."

Lady Carleton, nursing a red and swelling wrist, whirled on the earl. "Who are you?" she demanded furiously as her irate husband also added his voice to the query.

Fixing an icy stare on Sir Raymond, the earl said, "To the members of my family and to my friends, I am Richard Neville. To you, I am the Earl of Aylsford."

"Aylsford . . . Aylsford, by God, I have heard that name!" Sir Raymond growled. "You . . . you are a member of the Prince Regent's set. A rake, and deep in debt. That is common knowledge."

"I was," Richard responded coldly. Then, with an impish smile, he turned to Julie. "I had no idea that my fame had reached into so many unlikely quarters, my love."

"Why are you here?" Sir Raymond demanded. "And what have you to do with my sister?"

"He is here, Raymond," Julie said softly and just a little sadly, "because when I was not entirely sure of my reception, I entertained the notion that you might want to meet my husband."

"Your husband!" Sir Raymond glared at her. "You are married to . . . to this fortune hunter?"

"No," Julie said evenly, "I have not married a fortune hunter. Richard has no need to hunt a fortune,

Raymond. He has found it. I have already deeded all that I possess to him."

"That can be set aside," Lady Carleton shrilled. "You are mad . . . you are incompetent, you little wretch, and—"

"That is enough!" The earl, his eyes blazing, moved foward.

Julie, her hand on her husband's arm, said coldly, "Since it was through my advice that my father realized a sum which you as well as I have enjoyed, and will continue to enjoy, I must disagree with you. However, my dear Alicia, you are welcome to believe as you choose."

"You lie!" Sir Raymond shouted. "It was our father and none other made the investments that increased our fortune, you conniving little—"

The earl stepped foward hastily to confront Sir Raymond. Ignoring Julie's alarmed protest, he said sternly. "If you say anything more regarding my wife, Sir Raymond, I will be constrained to call you out, as I had actually wanted to do when I first heard this sorry tale. I was dissuaded from that plan by your much-injured sister." He paused and then continued disgustedly, "I might add that I did not quite believe all that she had told me—mainly because, loving her as much as I do and knowing her character through and through, I could not imagine that you and your siblings, being aware of how very much she has suffered already, could possibly have treated her so cruelly. Now that I have seen and met you for myself, I think, indeed, she must have softened her version of the events attendant upon her being forced to flee her own house. We will bid you good afternoon."

They were away from the Manor and turning into the little house where Lucy lived with her parents before Richard calmed down.

"To . . . to suggest that I married you for the money I

didn't even know you possessed! To suggest that anyone having the privilege of knowing you would care whether you were rich or poor! I have always counted myself unfortunate because I had neither sister nor brother and had to grow up by myself—but were I saddled with such a band of miscreants—" He came to an abrupt stop because Julie had gently placed her hand over his mouth.

"I think we need not speak of them again," she said softly. "I felt it was necessary to see them—in order to assure them that I was still alive, and I must admit that in spite of all that happened on that last night, I was foolish enough to think that they might be pleased to learn I was not dead, and to meet you, but just as I was dead to them—they are now dead to me. You are my whole family, Richard, my love."

"And you"—he gathered her into his arms—"are my life." He kissed her, and then, reluctantly releasing her, he said, "And now, let us fetch your abigail, my love, and, the Lord willing, we will be in London by late tomorrow."

"London?" Julie gazed at him in surprise. "We are going to London?"

He nodded, saying rather shortly, "I have unfinished business there. However, my dear love, I promise you that we'll not remain long—for I am in haste to show you Aylsford Keep."

"And I am in haste to see it!" she told him eagerly. "Imagine, a castle!"

"Imagine, the remains of a castle and a rather moldy house," he said ruefully. "My father, and his father before him, as well as myself . . . But I have told you all that."

She looked at him lovingly as she said gently, "I have no blame for you, Richard. Your estate was debt-ridden before you were born."

"The past does not excuse the present. However, my

Julie, I have hopes of doubling and even tripling the dowry you have brought me. I shall need your guidance, though."

"And will have it, of course, my dearest," she promised softly. There was no reason to let him know that she wished he would exclude London from their route. He did not have the memories of the city that she held. Yet, he had told her that he had no love for it either.

"I think of it as late nights at the tables in one or another hell, as drinking myself into oblivion, as betting on which turkey can run the fastest. I went the whole round, buying swift horses at Tattersall's, drinking 'blue ruin' at some Covent Garden gin shop, and . . . But I'll not weary you with these grim tales of my dissipations. My only saving grace was that I did not have enough of the ready to overindulge, and nor did I really have the inclination. I bought my yacht from Cary Gilchrist, who sold it so that he might enjoy London's streets rather than her waterways, poor lad. The last I heard of him, he was rotting in the Fleet. His fate frightened me." He had sighed, and then ashamedly he had told her that he intended to marry Diana mainly because he needed her dowry to pay off his debts.

He had told her all that before she brought him to Brighton, had told her, too, a plan of going to Canada, where he had property. He had asked her if she would mind living in the New World.

She would not have minded—but she had a feeling that he would have minded terribly, selling his estate. It was then that she had told him about her funds in the Brighton bank and over his oft-repeated objections insisted on incorporating them into the dowry he protested he did not want.

Consequently, why was he so insistent that they go to London—since he seemed to like it even less than she did. Probably there were debts he wanted to settle, or . . . But she decided not to ask him.

Three days later, Julie was still asking herself that question that had piqued her curiosity on the day they had stopped to fetch a delighted and tearful Lucy. They had remained in the city no longer than a day and a night, a period Richard agreed was far too long.

"I have come to realize that I much prefer the country," he had told her as they rolled out of the city. Yet, despite his oft-expressed contention that his former existence was anathema, he had shown a strong interest in its so-called bible, the *Morning Post,* with its gossipy tales of the *ton.*

They had stopped at village after village so that Richard might purchase and scan the paper. This morning was no different. They were now in the village of Hexham, more than three-quarters of the way to his castle, and she vainly trying to keep her impatience from showing.

Now, looking out the window of the Golden Horse, the inn where they had stopped for breakfast, and from which they should have already departed, in order to be on the road by now, she saw him striding back, a strange expression on his face, or rather, it was not strange, not exactly. She had discerned the same look when they left the Manor. "Grim" was the only way to describe it. But why was Richard looking so grim? He had a newspaper clutched in one hand. The *Morning Post?* Had he found the item for which he had obviously been searching?

She hurried to the door of the inn with Lucy's protest echoing in her ears. "You should not go out there alone, Miss . . . er, milady."

Ignoring the girl, she opened the door and came out to wait for Richard, who was only a few steps away.

"And who are you, my lovely?" came an appreciative

question voiced by a man standing a few feet away.

"Her identity need not concern you, sir," the earl said coldly.

"And I'd like to know—" the young man began.

Julie ran to her husband, looking up at him anxiously. "Richard, what's amiss?" she asked nervously.

His expression as he looked down at her was a mixture of surprise and reproof. "Why are you out here alone, my love? Have I not told you that you must never . . ." He paused and glanced at the young man who had spoken to Julie and who was now retreating quickly. He added with some annoyance, "You open yourself to—"

"Oh, never mind him," Julie said impatiently. "Tell me instead, what is so very important about the *Morning Post*?"

His look had turned bland. "The . . . er . . . *Morning Post,* my dearest girl? Did I ever say it was *important* to me?"

"No!" she actually snapped at him. "But since we have been stopping at every inn along the route, or very nearly, just for you to glance at it and throw it away, I have become curious."

"Ah." He smiled at her. "You are very discerning. Will you always continue to amaze me?" His smile had become a grin.

"And will you always tease me?" She actually stamped her foot. "Richard, you must tell me—"

"All in good time, my love," he said maddeningly, as, putting an arm around her, he escorted her back to the inn and to the table where she had been sitting with Lucy, who was still there shaking her head and looking anxious.

"That young man," she said. "I told you . . ." She bent a stern look on Julie.

"I am still in one piece, Lucy." Julie, looking at her husband, held out her hand. "Am I to see the newspaper?"

"You are, my love." He handed it to her. "You may sit here and read a certain item for yourself. It is on the second page, second column, third paragraph from the top. I suggest that you sit down."

"Very well, master of all masters." Julie took her seat at the table, and finding the item in question, was somewhat let down to discover that its headline read, "SHOCKING ATTACK ON M.P."

"A member of Parliament?" Julie raised wide eyes to the earl. "Why . . . ?"

"I beg you will read this short effusion," he said with just a touch of impatience.

"Very well," Julie replied.

The article was brief and beguilingly succinct. It read:

Sir Edwin Fitzroy, member from Canterbury, on his way to keep an appointment in the neighborhood of St. James's Square, was set upon by a madman brandishing a horsewhip. Without warning, the maniac leapt at him and struck him many times, leaving him in a most deplorable condition—bleeding from several places on back and face.

Sir Edwin, found insensible, is now recuperating in his home. The Bow Street Runners were dispatched to get a description of the attacker. Unfortunately, Sir Edwin has been unable to provide one.

The paper fell from Julie's nerveless grasp. "This . . . is what you have been hoping to find?"

He was looking grim again. "Yes, my love, this is the article that I have been hoping to find."

"You . . . knew of it—the attack, I mean?" Julie demanded confusedly. "How . . . ?"

"I knew of it," he said.

Something in his expression and in his tone of voice caused her to stare at him quizzically. "Richard," she whispered, "it was not . . . it could not have been *you*?"

Meeting her candid gaze, he said. "There are many inaccuracies in that account—all of them, I have no doubt, invented by the member from Canterbury. He was not horsewhipped in the vicinity of St. James's Square, but in his own library. His wife, fortunately, was in the country. I offered him swords or pistols, but he cravenly refused to duel with me. Consequently, I had no choice."

"No . . . choice," she whispered.

"He had to be punished," the earl said very grimly. "You see, my dearest love, I know a gentleman named Sir James Massinger, and one night when he was in his cups, he told me a tale that he found highly amusing. It was about an innocent young lady who, at her husband's express wish, was given spiked champagne by Sir James, who was well paid for his part in the plot . . ."

"The plot?" she whispered.

"Hear me, my angel. I will tell you the whole of it. I did not immediately connect you with that sorry tale. I had heard it a long time ago, but gradually it came back to me and I realized just what had happened and I resolved to get even . . . for you. Your onetime husband, my own, has a very short memory—as well he might, since he was party to a confidence."

"A confidence?" she questioned.

"A confidence," he repeated with considerable satisfaction. "And that was: unless he wanted to risk a repeat performance, he had best forget who it was that attacked him, and for what reason. Judging from that masterly item, he has done just that. And now, my dearest love, I am most eager to show you the Keep, so let us be on our way.''

"Oh, Richard, I . . . I am without words," she whispered.

"Words are not needed at this present moment," he said masterfully. Removing the paper from her clutch, and quite unmindful of Lucy, a silent listener to his tale, he bent to kiss his wife passionately—to the considerable enjoyment and envy of several gentlemen who had just descended from the same coach that had brought the *Morning Post*.

Epilogue

The castle, constructed in the fourteenth century, had once been surrounded by a moat, but that had been filled in once Border disputes were settled by words rather than swords. Trees grew where war machines had been drawn up to shell the tall, broken Keep. Dark green vines covered its shattered walls, and moss grew in the crevices between the bricks, with occasionally a hardy daisy shoving its white-and-yellow head out for a brief springtime blooming.

Hard by the tower rose the mansion, still known as Aylsford Keep. It had been built by the third earl in the year 1672, when with a grant from Charles II he had amassed enough money either to restore the castle, wrecked and pillaged by the Puritans, or to construct a new house. He had decided on the latter, and designed it himself with the help of his countess. It was she who had also planned the great spread of gardens with their fountains, grottoes, streams, and a small lake.

The gardens were particularly beautiful in the summer, and the present Countess of Aylsford was delighted to show her guests through them. They had admired the Italian garden, had been pleasantly confused during a walk through the maze, and had greatly admired a vista which, Lady Revell said, rivaled anything designed by the great Capability Brown. Now they were sitting in a little latticed summerhouse near the lake, idly watching three swans gliding past, and on the shore, several drakes pruning their iridescent green feathers.

"Well." Lady Revell, a small, vivacious woman of some twenty-eight years, smiled as she thrust a hand through her dark curls, pushing them out of her face. "I have heard that you were a financial wizard, Lady Julie, but I can see that you have magic in your fingers as well, if your husband is to be believed. Did you really design the whole of the gardens?"

Julie rolled her eyes. "If he said that, he will be haunted, and rightly so, by the spirits of several angry ancestors as well as one of his paternal aunts!" She glanced at her lord, how sitting across from them and deep in a low-voiced conversation with Sir Anthony Revell. "Richard is inclined to exaggerate. The gardens were beautiful when I first came here. The maze was planned when the new house was built, and the lake has been here longer than either the house or the old Keep. I did redesign the Italian garden after we returned from Rome—two years ago. I had fallen in love with the Borghese Gardens, you see. Richard was fortunate enough to have an acquaintanceship with the English ambassador, who, in turn, knew the prince, and so we were shown through them."

"Oh, they must have been lovely!" Lady Revell exclaimed. She added with a giggle, "It was a pity that you missed seeing Pauline Bonaparte Borghese, or should I call her the 'princess?' Is a princess a princess when she is divorced? No matter, I hear she shocked Parisian society by posing nearly in the nude for the sculptor Canova. She thought nothing of it, I might add. 'There was a fire in the room,' was all she said to the scandalmongers."

Julie laughed. "She is the only one of the Bonapartes that I should like to meet."

"That notorious woman?" Lady Revell said in feigned shock. "I am surprised at you."

"But we are both notorious," Julie murmured.

"Nonsense, you are received everywhere—divorce or no divorce—and all the *ton* is quite aware why a certain gentleman was horsewhipped, and by whom. *He* is not received, and neither is his wife."

"That is hardly fair." Julie frowned. "I am sure she had nothing to do with it."

"And I am sure that she did," Lady Revell said frankly. "That is the *on-dit.*"

"Come, come, I cannot believe that anyone still remembers so ancient a scandal!" Julie protested.

"Oh, my dear, all the old scandals get an airing when there is nothing new to titillate a jaded ear—I have learned that since we have been residing in London. Can you imagine that every so often someone will bring up Georgiana, Duchess of Devonshire, and the fact that she shared the duke with her best friend, who subsequently married his grace—hardly waiting until poor Georgiana was cold in her grave? And then there is Caroline Lamb and her chasing after Lord Byron . . . and of course, there is Byron's wife, the graceless Annabelle, and his sister Augusta—no wonder the poor man prefers to live in Italy. But enough! Tell me more about the gardens. I am so anxious to travel abroad, and I should adore to visit Rome. I am utterly fascinated by antiquities, at least those I see in the British Museum. Tell me more about Rome, too!"

"Rome, well . . . Rome is Rome." Julie smiled. "My descriptions could never approach its reality. Suffice to say that 'magnificent' is too small a word to encompass it. You will have to go and see it for yourself."

"I will go," Lady Revell said decisively. "Anthony has promised that we will—but he has failed to tell me when. Still, you may be assured that I intend to hold him to that promise."

"I am quite willing to be held to it, my dear Celia."
Sir Anthony visited a fond smile upon his wife's lively
countenance. "We would have gone earlier this year
had we not been summoned home to Cornwall for your
sister Kitty's wedding." He fell back into conversation
with the earl, while Lady Revell, lowering her voice,
said, "I owe you a great debt, you know. In fact, you
are inadvertently responsible for all my present happiness."

"I?" Julie looked at her blankly.

"Love . . ." There was a faint note of protest in Sir
Anthony's tone as he broke off mid-conversation to
visit a reproachful glance on his wife's animated face.

"You are not supposed to be listening to me," she
reproved. "You are being rude to your host."

"I must beg to differ with you." The earl smiled. "I
find myself extremely curious. What manner of debt
can you owe to my wife?"

"Oh dear, oh dear," Lady Revell laughed. "Will you
tell me that you, too, were listening? Very well, you
shall know, even though Anthony does not like to talk
about it." She turned her merry eyes on Julie again.
"He fell madly in love with you, my dear Lady Julie,
you know."

"Celia!" Sir Anthony protested, and grimaced.

"Dear, dear, what a dreadful face! Still, I refuse to be
put off by it. I will continue with my story."

"Please do," Julie urged, "though I am sure you are
exaggerating when you say that he fell in love with me."

"No, I am not," Lady Revell said firmly. "He did
fall in love with you, and before that, the thought
himself passionately in love with that abandoned
creature Diana, and when he met me . . . well, he told
me quite frankly that there was something about me
that reminded him of you—though I really cannot see it
myself, save that we are both small. You are so very
beautiful and I do envy you your golden hair! However,

it was you who did make him fall out of love with Diana, and does she not deserve her fate!"

"Her fate?" Julie questioned.

"I very much doubt that she would term it a 'fate,' my love." Sir Anthony grinned. "She might not be a titled lady, but she does seem tolerably happy despite her present situation."

"On the days that he does not beat her." Lady Revell rolled her eyes.

"Or she him." Her husband winked.

"What is this you are saying?" The earl raised his eyebrows. "We had heard from Sir Nigel that his daughter married a sea captain, a man of whom he did not seem to quite approve." He looked at Julie. "When did we receive that letter, my love? It was quite some time ago, as I recall."

"I am sure that it must have been," Lady Revell said frankly.

"Oh?" Julie gave her an anxious look. "I do hope that he is well."

"He is very well indeed." Lady Revell giggled. "Diana, however, is another matter. The man she married, one Jonathan Rudd by name—and manner, I might add—does own a ship, a yacht rechristened the *Diana,* but he does not precisely qualify as a sea captain, at least not in the Royal Navy."

"He is a smuggler," Sir Anthony said bluntly. "But he is rich enough and well-connected enough—at least with the militia and some few justices of the peace, so-called, to stay out of prison. However, it is common knowledge that he barely missed being transported to New South Wales. That was several years ago, of course, while we were still at war with France. I would say that a goodly lot of French brandy was stowed beneath some judicial benches."

"He is a real rogue, as you must have guessed," Lady Revell said. "However, as my husband was just saying, he is rich—very rich, which is well for our proud Diana. She, you see, was disinherited shortly before the birth of her first child.''

"Good God, why?'' the earl demanded. "That does not sound like Sir Nigel.''

"I believe,'' Lady Revell explained with no little relish, "that he was exercised over the fact that our rogue had not yet wed our Diana. However, he did rectify that oversight in time to declare the babe legitimate if not premature. Since then, his lady wife has presented him with two more children. And—''

"She has three children—already?'' Julie demanded in some surprise.

"She has them, I have heard, with amazing ease, and she appears to be a good mother. She is often seen riding in the vicinity of her old home with one or another of her brood up before her in the saddle, and her rapscallion of a husband keeping pace with her on a huge chestnut stallion. Occasionally she will have a black eye, or so will he. They have had some wild set-tos at one or another Helston tavern, with the more sporting citizens laying odds on who will fall first. Then, more often than not, they break out laughing, embrace in the most wanton way, order drinks all around, and go off as happily as if they had not been threatening each other with instant extinction.'' She giggled.

"You should not laugh at them, my love,'' Sir Anthony reproved with mock solemnity. "Their exploits are of considerable embarrassment to her father and his wife—for nearly every time they are seen around Excalibur Hall, they are three-parts drunk. Married or single, Diana remains a handful for her father.''

"Did you say . . . his wife?'' Julie demanded excitedly. Without giving Sir Anthony a chance to reply, she continued, "You will not be telling us that Sir Nigel has married again?''

"Oh, did he not write to let you know? But you say

that you've not heard from him," Lady Revell commented. "I think that he has become neglectful of these little chores, mainly because he is so very happy. They had a long honeymoon in Greece, and a few months after they returned, she bore him a son. The child is named after his father. He is adorable. Theresa is a very sweet woman—that is Lady Penrose's given name. She is the widow of one of his old school friends. Imagine, she and Sir Nigel met at her husband's funeral."

"That is not what I would call a very romantic spot," the earl commented.

"My love," his wife said gently, "we are hardly in the place to make such an assessment."

His eyes widened and filled with laughter. "You are entirely right, my sweet. I fell in love with a girl clinging to a capsized rowboat."

"You did not!" she contradicted. "Not then."

"Well, not very long afterward," he said firmly. "But this current situation. You must tell me about it, Lady Revell. How is it possible that if she was the widow of his old friend, they had never met before the funeral?"

"The way I understand it," Lady Revell said, "is that they had been good friends—but Nigel's friend was a diplomat and stationed abroad. However, he had a home near Excalibur Hall and he moved back there shortly before he became ill. He had every intention of renewing the friendship . . . but it was too late."

"Oh dear, what a pity," Julie sighed.

"Yes, indeed. I understand he was a very nice man," Lady Revell said.

"His wife must be much younger than Sir Nigel," the earl commented.

"No, she was forty-three when they married. She has two grown children from her first marriage. However, I do not think she will have any more. Even if she could, Sir Nigel would not allow it. He was terribly worried about her condition. Now, you should see him. He adores the child. He's a wonderful father."

"A very indulgent father." The earl frowned. "I hope he does not spoil him. Certainly he spoiled Diana."

"Undoubtedly, he did. I think, however, that he has learned his lesson. Still, it is difficult not to pamper an only child. I did my share of that before I had my second boy." Lady Revell smiled at her husband and then turned wide eyes on Julie. "And your daughter is adorable . . ."

"Shhh." Julie cast a mischievous look at her husband and put a finger to her lips.

"What did I say?" Lady Revell whispered.

"Which reminds me, my love," the earl said. "I do think we have been out here long enough. You have not yet had your afternoon rest."

"Oh, Richard, I am not in the least tired," Julie assured him. "And I have not been doing anything active. I have only been sitting here quietly in the summerhouse."

"And before that, you took a long tour of the gardens," he reminded her.

"That is certainly not taxing. I walked very slowly."

Lady Revell had been looking confused, but now she looked at her hostess. "You will never be telling me—" she began.

"In eight months . . . *eight,*" Julie said with a slightly exasperated look at her husband. "And Richard is acting as if it were but eight days! Furthermore, as I must continually remind him, the second birth is easier than the first. I will match Diana in that."

"You match her in nothing," the earl said fiercely. "You surpass her in everything."

"Not if she has three children, already," Julie said teasingly.

"You are not running races with her, my love. Furthermore, this child, I think, will be our last. This is the second time we have disappointed poor David and postponed our voyage to Canada."

"David? That is your nephew, Julie?" Sir Anthony inquired.

"He is," Julie confirmed.

"I admit to curiosity," Sir Anthony pursued. "Why would you be disappointing your nephew?"

"Because he and his wife look to us to bring them news of London, and also because, as we understand it, he has created a small paradise out of the acres Richard gave him," Julie said proudly. "We will go eventually."

Lady Revell looked surprised. "I thought you were completely out of touch with your family. You will never tell me that you have mended matters, and after all—"

"No," Julie interrupted quickly. "I will certainly never tell you that. My sisters have made overtures of peace since my marriage"—she grimaced—"but I fear I have ignored them. David is another matter entirely. Though he's the eldest son of my brother Raymond, he, too, is out of touch and in deep disgrace." She shook her head. "He has been for years."

"Oh, now I do remember." Lady Revell nodded. "Anthony did tell me that he was the Good Samaritan who helped you out of your window and into a waiting coach."

"Yes," Julie acknowledged softly. "Indeed, he is inadvertently responsible for all that happened after I traveled or, rather, fled to Brighton."

"Hold my love," the earl complained. "Had I no share in that?"

"You have had the lion's share, my dearest." Julie gave him a fond look. "However, as you well know, were it not for David, we would never have met. You must keep that in mind."

"It is not I who must keep it in mind, it is you." He smiled. "We will have to make that visit next year."

"Have David's parents never forgiven him?" Lady Revell asked interestedly.

"No, they have not," Julie sighed.

"In fact," the earl commented, "they have inked his name from the family Bible."

"He is disinherited?" Lady Revell asked.

The earl shook his head. "They tried to disinherit him, but that proved impossible thanks to the law of primogeniture. He is the only son and he will inherit the Manor and title."

"If he chooses," Julie said. "He might prefer to stay in Canada. He loves the country, and they live near the town of York, which he insists will be a great city one day. He enjoys the life, and of course Natalie, his wife, has never known any other. She is Canadian born."

"At any rate, that decision will not need to be made for many years, I should imagine," Lady Revell commented.

"That is debatable," the earl said. "My wife's brother Raymond is over fifty and happens to have a most choleric disposition, one that has not been improved by a series of highly injudicious investments— so says Mr. Soames, our man of business. He does not have his little sister's talent for high finance."

"I am sure that has not improved his disposition," Julie sighed. "Mr. Soames says that his buying and selling are highly erratic, and I should not be surprised if he were egged on by his wife."

"She must be a horror!" Lady Revell exclaimed.

"Yes," Julie agreed. "Raymond was very kind to me when I was younger. I lay his defection at Alicia's door. She and I were never in sympathy."

"Nonsense!" Lady Revell cried. "I do not wish to

disillusion you further about your brother, my dear, but a woman can only do so much. The burden rests securely on his shoulders, I'll be bound.''

"To the contrary, my dearest Celia, a woman can do a very great deal.'' Sir Anthony smiled at his wife.

"I should know that,'' the earl agreed with a long look at Julie. "Particularly this woman . . . she is an alchemist.''

"An alchemist?'' Lady Revell demanded lightly. "Have you yet another talent up your sleeve, Lady Julie?''

"My husband is teasing,'' Julie laughed.

"Not at all, my darling. You *are* an alchemist—for you have changed the dross of my existence into the very purest gold.''

"My love, you grow extravagant.'' Julie smiled and blushed. "Whatever will our guests think?''

"Speaking for myself and, I am sure, for my husband also,'' Lady Revell said, "I would think that you are both in the process of living happily ever after.''